# Rotten Dates

*A Carol Sabala Mystery*

Vinnie Hansen

*Rotten Dates*
A Carol Sabala Mystery

This is a work of fiction. While some real Santa Cruz locations have been used, they have been used fictitiously, and therefore I have taken small liberties. All the characters and incidents in this work are products of the author's imagination. Any resemblance to actual persons, living or dead, or actual events is entirely coincidental.

Cover art by Book Cover Corner, www.bookcovercorner.com

Background cover artwork: Daniel S. Friedman

ISBN-10: 0-9974674-0-1

ISBN-13: 978-0-9974674-0-6

Hansen, Vinnie.

Rotten Dates / Vinnie Hansen — 2nd ed.

*For "The Kids," Kimiye & Justin*

# PRAISE FOR HANSEN'S WORK

*"With edgy precision, Hansen applies all the elements of a good mystery: interesting plot, compelling characters, a finely drawn sense of place, and excellent writing.* One Tough Cookie *has made me a fan, one who can't wait to gorge on* Rotten Dates.*"*
--Denise Osborne, author of *Feng Shui Mysteries*
and Queenie Davilov Mysteries

*Black Beans & Venom* – Claymore Award Finalist and B.R.A.G. Medallion recipient.

*"Her writing style is like liquid poetry. Her characters rule the page, and the action moves smoothly from one scene to the next."*
Midwest Book Review

*"I love Carol Sabala...quirky, gutsy and my kind of gal in an aqua tank top."*
--Cara Black, Author of the Aimée Leduc mystery series

*"Hansen's sense of humor and protagonist make for a good read. I particularly enjoyed her faithfully rendered Santa Cruz background."*
--Laura Crum, author of the Gail McCarthy murder mystery series

*"The pacing of Hansen's story is excellent."*
--Chris Watson, *Santa Cruz Sentinel* on *Murder, Honey*

*"I just finished* Murder, Honey *and I found it splendid."*
--Laura Davis, author of *Courage to Heal*

*"In Sabala, Hansen has created a likable sleuth whose many problems readers may readily identify with, and as far as Carol's mother goes—well, let's just say I hope we see more of her in the future."*
--Michael Cornelius, *The Bloomsbury Review*

*"Five silver pens out of five for '*Tang Is Not Juice.*'"*
--Silas Spaeth, *Salinas Californian*

*"Best Book of Fiction of 2005" for* Tang Is Not Juice
Oklahoma Writers' Federation, Inc.

## ALSO BY VINNIE HANSEN:

Murder, Honey

One Tough Cookie

Squeezed & Juiced

Death with Dessert

Art, Wine & Bullets

Black Beans & Venom

# SEPTEMBER, 1995

# CHAPTER 1

With a growing pool of dread in my stomach, I wove through Santa Cruz's tourist-clogged streets in my rusty Ghia.

In the passenger seat, Suzanne read aloud. "Divorced white male, forty-two, rich, handsome, brown, brown, six feet of solid muscle ready to satisfy your every desire. Has a brain, too. In search of a fit, pretty woman thirty to forty. Call now. Won't last."

At a traffic light, I glanced over at the local rag she held out to me. The actual text looked like hieroglyphics: *DWM, 42, rich, hdsm., br.br.6' . . . Call now.*

The "won't last" had been Suzanne's little improvisation. She aimed a dazzling smile at me. "Perfect, Carol."

"Not if he *won't last*." The light changed and I inched forward. The idea of dating seemed as oppressive as the steamy weather.

Suzanne wrinkled her nose at me. Her golden shoulders glowed in the sunshine glinting through her window. My friend had been unfairly endowed: a five-foot-six body that stayed slim regardless of what she ate or did, tawny curly hair, flawless skin, and sweet amber eyes. And, most obnoxious of all, the sweetness was sincere.

I switched lanes to avoid getting stuck behind a crosstown bus up ahead. The muscles in my face set like concrete. Stubborn my mom would call me. Too stubborn to be born.

"What makes you think I need a man?" I finally asked.

"Okay. How 'bout a woman?" she asked brightly.

Painful as this conversation was, it was preferable to following my thoughts toward my mom, who had recently decided to retire to Santa Cruz.

"Look," Suzanne campaigned. "You and Chad haven't slept together since you asked him for a divorce, right?"

I ignored her. Chad had been annoyingly accommodating about our separation.

"So that's been--what? Six months?"

"Something like that." In fact, the divorce had sailed cheaply through a legal service, with little acrimony and less delay.

At the next light, I glanced at the paper again and plunked my finger on an ad. "Here's a good one for me." I leaned over to read "Mr. Wrong" followed by a number.

Suzanne's eyes laughed at me across the small space.

I picked up the flowered scrunchie Suzanne had deposited between us. Blanketed by my auburn hair, my neck felt as though I were in a steam room. I lifted the heavy mane and fastened it into a ponytail with Suzanne's ruffled band.

This amused her, too. "Hot?" The innuendo dripped like the sweat on my neck.

We crawled forward. Suzanne was paving my road to hell with good intentions.

"Look, the dates are cheap." she continued her relentless encouragement. "Just coffee or something like that. It's an adventure. And it's safe."

I'm sure that statement later haunted Suzanne's conscious mind and reverberated in her nightmares. Even as she said it, she shivered, despite the sun boiling us like a couple of lobsters.

We passed the Santa Cruz institutions of India Joze and the Goodwill. Anything that still occupied the same building after the 1989 earthquake counted as an institution to me. My mom had been delighted to find a Goodwill only blocks from her new home.

I followed the curve of Chestnut Street toward the Hinds House, a three-story, cream-colored Victorian where my mother had taken up residence. I wondered if she'd chosen it because our hometown of Ferndale, population 1,420, had been largely Victorians. Maybe she wished we'd lived in one.

The old Roaring Camp train came clanging by, and we waved at the tourists returning from the redwoods. Nearly all the passengers on the open car and at the windows of the enclosed cars waved back.

"Isn't it amazing what power we have," Suzanne said. "By simply moving our hand, we can get about fifty percent of those people to do the same."

Neither her charm nor my curiosity about the Romance Connection ads could allay my growing apprehension as we neared the historic house. Buff and dark brown trim accented the bay windows and ran in fretwork around the cornice and second-floor balcony. Terrace Hill rose behind the Victorian.

I miraculously found a parking space a few doors down.

"So?" Suzanne said.

"So what?"

"So look at you."

I scrounged in my purse and pulled out a mirror, a rectangular job with a bank's advertisement on the maroon plastic case. To be sarcastic, I inspected myself. Bags puffed under my blue-green eyes. "Why didn't you tell me that I had flour up my nose?" This was a baker's occupational hazard.

"Sorry I didn't bother to check your nostrils. If this doesn't prove my point, Carol, I don't know what does."

I was unaware that Suzanne had made a point, but in spite of the current, elliptical conversation, she was not the stereotype of a dumb blonde. The *garde manger*, Suzanne was easily the most sensible person in the kitchen at Archibald's, where we both worked. "I can see me meeting this handsome, satisfy-all-your-desires stud," I said. "He'd look at my nostrils and hand me a spoonful of cocaine."

"There's a pay phone over by the Goodwill."

"Geez and my mom thinks *I'm* stubborn."

"I'm not stubborn," Suzanne said. "I'm persistent. And you're not stubborn either, just in need of a good lay."

"You want to tell that to my mom?"

"Let's get out of this car. I'm dying."

Getting out of the car did not provide me any relief. We mounted the steps.

"Why are you so nervous?"

"I'm not nervous," I snapped.

"Nor horny."

The heavy, carved door had a key in its center that one turned to ring the chime.

"How many people live here?" Suzanne asked.

"I don't know. I think my mom said there are eleven rooms."

I knocked and twisted the key again.

"Relax," Suzanne whispered.

The man who filled the open door was hearty, blond and about forty. "Good afternoon," he said. "May I help you?"

I was a sucker for accents. I also liked dress shirts with the sleeves rolled up and the top button opened. By the way Suzanne was staring, so did she.

"My mom lives here," I explained.

"That must be the charming Bea Sabala," he said. "My neighbor." He made a little bow and waved us in.

Surely nobody, not even my dad in their courting days, had called my mom *charming*. Smart, brave, good-looking. I could imagine a thesaurus of adjectives for my mom, but not *charming*. She had as much charm as you'd expect from a person who'd spent her life scraping tartar from teeth.

"Your mother is having a bath," the dimpled hunk said. "I am Klaus Holthuis."

I trembled like a schoolgirl as he extended his hand. He had a firm, warm handshake that stayed engaged a second too long. His hair was not blond, but gold, his eyes a slate blue and appraising, his shoes sturdy brown leather, well crafted and European.

"Suzanne Anderson," Suzanne said, thrusting out her hand and breaking up my reverie.

"A pleasure to meet you."

I felt like jamming my elbow into Suzanne's ribs and declaring, "I saw him first."

Klaus led us around a huge bouquet of red roses in the middle of the commodious entryway. The parlors on both sides of the entrance featured wainscoting, wallpaper, fireplaces, stained glass and thick rugs on the wooden floors. The house was quiet, as though occupied only by my mother and Klaus. The aroma of fresh coffee swirled around the foyer.

"Would you care to join me for coffee while you wait for your mother?"

I'd just finished a mug of French roast and Suzanne didn't drink coffee, but we bobbed our heads like a pair of trained parakeets.

He led us back to a kitchen that seemed funky compared to the elegant front rooms. He gestured for us to sit at a round table while he rustled up three mugs, with no protest from little Ms. Anderson about the evils of caffeine.

"I take it black," I said.

"A woman after my own heart," Klaus said.

"Black for me, too," Suzanne said.

I shot her daggers, but she looked as though she could barely stifle laughter. "I told you so," her eyes said. "Horny, horny, horny."

Klaus delivered the three coffees and sat down with us. "Has anyone ever told you," he said, gazing at me, "that you have a very beautiful . . ."

I held my breath. My heart palpitated. I felt like a heroine in a romance novel.

" . . . neck," he concluded.

My fluttering spark was ground out with a boot tip. *Neck.* Unless you were a tribal woman in Africa, where a neck stretched with loop after loop of jewelry was considered sexy, who wanted a guy to notice her neck?

"Thanks," I mumbled.

My mother entered the kitchen looking rosy from her bath. I stood to greet her, glad to escape the unwanted coffee and the painful letdown.

At her prime, my mom had been five foot four, but now she'd started to shrink, and I was a head taller than she was. She tipped up the bill of a John Deere cap, and inspected all of us as though we were salesmen. In spite of the warmth of the day, she wore a crocheted, chartreuse vest over her clothes. I glanced at Suzanne and Klaus to see if they were smirking, but my mom's demeanor squelched any such impulse.

I introduced her to Suzanne.

"Nice to meet you, Mrs. Sabala," Suzanne said.

"Bea," my mom said.

My mom's knitted, florescent orange slippers with pompoms screamed for attention.

I didn't mind that my mom crocheted and knitted. She had made me lovely throws. She'd also made me macabre throws. It wasn't the crocheting, but her Child-of-The-Great-Depression mentality and lack of patience that were the problems. She bought her yarn at garage sales and she let no color go to waste. She didn't wait for a new yard sale to produce complementary shades. She used whatever yarn she had on hand, creating original, sometimes disturbing combinations.

In the past, I'd given away her more creative presents to thrift shops. Now that my mom lived in Santa Cruz, I'd have to devise a more ingenious disposal, just one way that life was folding around me, as though I were the center of some origami project.

"You really lucked out," Suzanne said to my mom. "This place is beautiful."

"Shallow men believe in luck," my mom said.

With a drop of satisfaction, I watched Suzanne stiffen. Maybe now she'd understand why I'd dreaded this visit, and why my mom's relocation had thrown me into a depression.

"Mom's just quoting someone," I said.

Now my mother looked offended, her wrinkled face as sad as a basset hound's. "I did my homework to find this place. It wasn't luck."

I sighed. Santa Cruz *was* a great place for seniors—temperate weather, progressive programs, and fairly good public transportation. The latter was important since my mom had recently mistaken her gas pedal for her brake and had driven into the Ferndale Post Office. No one had been injured and her insurance had covered the damage, but the experience had been humiliating for my mom, and the settlement had left her with no driver's license. The incident was her prime reason for leaving Ferndale, and her only remaining child was her prime reason for moving to Santa Cruz.

"Do you want to show me your room, Mom?"

My mom tugged at the collar of the plaid, flannel shirt under her chartreuse vest. She scratched her clavicle.

"I'll wait here," Suzanne volunteered.

By the time I returned, she'd have Klaus enthralled. For a second, I wished she were dead. Or, at least, invisible.

"The t.v. room has Showtime," my mom told Suzanne.

As we walked side-by-side up the wide staircase, my mother added, "Lovely girl. I'll give you some slippers for her." She paused on the second floor. "Five bigger rooms here."

We continued. I didn't voice my concern about her climbing two flights of stairs on a regular basis. My mom would dismiss my worry. One needed daily exercise. Nothing I said was ever right. I stuck to the safe, boring, informational conversation my mom preferred. My former mother-in-law had been clingy, dependent, and manipulative. My mother was critical, independent, and blunt. I wasn't sure at the moment which mother was more difficult.

The landing of the third floor contained a counter with a sink, microwave, and small refrigerator, so at least my mom wouldn't have to run up and down the steps every time she wanted a cup of tea. I was glad for my own sake, too, since I could already feel the ache under my kneecaps.

"My room's an atelier," my mom pronounced carefully, like a word she'd only recently learned. She opened a door to the right. "Used to be part of the attic."

The room was the size of a tract house bedroom, and the ceiling slanted toward the far wall.

"Don't bump your head."

I sat in a wicker chair. My mom had placed pictures of Donald and me as babies on a vanity with beveled glass, and her crocheted pillows and throws announced her presence to a room full of wicker furniture, an armoire, and a tole lamp.

"The room is furnished," my mom explained unnecessarily. She plopped on a bench by the vanity. In an alcove beside her, a narrow window opened into the room and above me a small skylight allowed additional light.

"What did you do with our stuff?" I both didn't care and cared intensely. Our home near Ferndale had been a hideously middle-class ranch-style house, with a plaid couch and matching wing chairs. But, nonetheless it was my childhood home.

"Estate sale. Storage."

My mom did nothing to comfort me. She never had. She didn't reassure me that she'd kept sentimental items. I wasn't sure my mom knew the concept of sentimental. She didn't ask about the divorce or how I was doing. Instead she said, "Mostly professors or graduate students visiting UCSC stay here."

"That sounds good."

"Yes." She reflected. She pointed to the small television by the bed. "That has cable, too." She instantly retreated to her pursed lip, philosophic mode. "The tenant next to me, the guy you met in the kitchen, seems a little strange."

"Strange?"

"She flipped the bill of her hat up and down, eyed the opened window above her door, and cleared her throat.

"Strange how, Mom?"

She stood and pushed up on a thin rod, which shut the window. Then she whispered, "Sexually." She strangled on the word.

# CHAPTER 2

Suzanne put the florescent orange slippers over her hands like puppets and made them growl at me.

"Very cute," I snarled. The visit with my mom had done nothing to relieve my churlish mood. I flipped an illegal U turn and headed straight out of the Hinds House down Church Street.

"So your mom thinks Klaus is a pervert?" Suzanne chirped.

"She didn't say that. Just that he was sexually strange. We're talking about a woman here who referred to my gay brother Donald as a bachelor even as he was dying of AIDS." As usual, the thought of my brother made my heart feel like a pincushion. I wondered if the pain would ever go away. At the same time, I hoped it never would. As long as I felt the pain, I remembered my brother. To stop hurting would seem like a betrayal.

"With my mom," I said, "sexually strange could mean the guy likes oral sex."

Suzanne averted her gaze to the low, white stucco buildings of City Hall. "What do you think she meant?"

"I don't know," I said. "She was practically apoplectic saying 'sexually.'"

"Then maybe it's not anything bad." She turned back to me. "Maybe you should try to hook up with this Klaus. You were practically drooling in the coffee."

"Right," I said. "Hook up with some guy who admires my neck and my mom thinks is weird."

Suzanne made one of the bright orange puppets nip at my

neck. "Yum, yum, yum. Maybe he has a neck fetish."

I jerked away from her, making the Ghia swerve. "Stop it."

She rolled her eyes, stripped the slippers from her hands, and jammed them into her gigantic, shoulder-strap leather purse, a relic, worn to a soft patina. "You definitely need to call that ad."

"Tell me that I should be happy to have my mother move to town."

"You should be happy your mother has moved to town. The slippers are the best conversation pieces I've had in weeks."

"This Romance Connection stuff couldn't be that hot then." I was getting tired of my own negativity. "Really, Suzanne," I said seriously, "if she were your mom, would you be happy?"

"I wouldn't mind because I have a life."

"So let's hear about this life."

"So let's go to Seabright Brewery."

If I left Suzanne, I'd be heading home to my little house in the sunny banana belt of Santa Cruz. It'd been too small for both Chad and me, but seemed vastly empty with only myself and Lola, my cat, so I gave in to frittering away the day.

Probably tired of my blistered seats poking her bare skin, Suzanne suggested we take her car. We made a pit stop on my cul-de-sac to switch to her yellow Volkswagen bug.

As a college town, Santa Cruz supported a large number of microbreweries. The appeal of Seabright Brewery was hard to discern at first. One got chilled by the ocean breeze, but couldn't see the ocean. As a matter of fact, the patio area looked out on railroad tracks. Still the place was packed in the late afternoon with a fortyish crowd.

We found two plastic chairs at an outside table. As soon as we ordered a Seabright Amber and a Pelican Pale, Suzanne resumed her campaign.

She spread the *Good Times* on the white table. "Call now."

"If I wanted to meet someone through advertising, I could

use the Internet." I was a technological moron, but my classes in criminology had warmed me to my computer. I would need it for locates and basic background searches.

"These ads are local and more effective."

"No way I'm going to answer an ad to find sex."

Suzanne's eyes stared down at the paper. Then she looked up at me, her face flushed even though the inland heat was sucking in the fog, which changed the temperature as quickly as an air conditioner. "It's working for me."

"You answered an ad!" This was a woman who stopped production whenever she walked across the kitchen at work.

"I answered one, but the guy didn't respond," Suzanne whispered, "so I decided to place one."

I snatched the *Good Times* and pulled it in front of me. "Is your ad in this week's?"

"Yeah," she said shyly.

"I can't believe you called and a guy didn't answer. If a guy didn't call you, why in the world do you think one would call me?"

I skimmed for Suzanne's ad. "There are way more Men Seeking Women than Women Seeking Men."

"See," she smiled. "The world is your oyster."

"Have you had lots of responses to your ad?"

"Lots."

The waitress plunked down menus and two sweating pints of beer. Suzanne automatically asked for fries. I didn't order anything. I hadn't had much appetite for months, but I kept the menu with the hope that springs eternal within the human breast.

"Ten?" I probed.

Suzanne sipped her light brew.

"Twenty?"

"Could I have my scrunchie?"

I let down my hair, gave my tresses a shake, and handed Suzanne the band. "More?"

"Maybe thirty."

A large pipe over the edge of the patio splashed water into a concrete receptacle, making a pleasant background noise.

"I don't get it." I continued skimming the columns. "The one guy you called, didn't call you, but you had like thirty responses to your ad?"

"He was probably in the situation I'm in now. Overwhelmed. Maybe he decided to investigate only the first ten callers." She shrugged. "Who knows? I don't give good phone."

I found Suzanne's ad: *sweet as anything I concoct with my AA in Culinary Arts.* She'd included the usual bare bones description and the type of man she wanted: 30-40, intelligent, fit, content with his life and able to laugh.

I liked the fact that she had no prescription for looks and noted that she had no prohibitions on meat, smoking, or drugs. Maybe she'd left the field too open.

"What's this last line about *frisky, tie the knot?*"

"Oh they screwed that part up," Suzanne said, grabbing at the paper. "Beverly told me I needed something to make me sound exciting."

I wasn't surprised Suzanne's cousin would recommend the word *frisky.*

"That last part is supposed to say *not ready to tie the knot,*" Suzanne explained.

"So how many of these guys have you actually met?"

"Maybe ten."

"And you already have a fantastic sex life?" My eyes switched to the greasy possibilities on the menu: buffalo wings, chili, and calamari.

"I exaggerated," Suzanne confessed. "But there's potential. No jerks yet, and I've met a person of interest." She wiggled her eyebrows at me.

The traffic on the street thickened with the rush hour. I jabbed the ads with my finger and swigged my dark, bitter beer.

"How much does it cost?"

Her eyes flickered with gold as she wound her curly hair on top her head and fastened it with her scrunchie.

"I'm just curious, Suzanne. I'm not going to do it."

"Hey, I visited your mom with you," she protested.

"You chickened out and enjoyed yourself with Klaus."

"There were no sparks between us," she reassured me. "I guess my neck is too short."

"At least you're not a giraffe. What kind of guy admires a neck?"

Carrying a tray of beers, the waitress handed off the basket of fries on her way to the next table. Suzanne drowned the thick brown potatoes with ketchup. I picked up a fry and slapped the coated end into my mouth.

"Klaus asked about you."

"He did?" The bubbling sensation in my body was completely out of whack with Suzanne's statement.

"He asked if you worked at Archibald's, too."

"What did you say?"

"Geez, Louise, what do you think? I said that you were the baker."

I felt ashamed. Even if you were the best baker at the fanciest restaurant, *baker* didn't carry much prestige or pizzazz, a heretofore unrealized motive for wanting to become a private investigator. I also felt my privacy violated. I didn't want Klaus to know where I worked. It not only diminished my mystery, but also provided a way to find out nearly everything about a person. As a snoop, I knew this.

"Was that all?" I asked.

"I guess. We chatted about the usual stuff. How does he like Santa Cruz, that kind of thing."

"Why wasn't he your type?"

She shrugged, tired of my grilling. "I don't know. He's the kind of guy who kept straightening the spoon on his napkin."

"That's it? That's all it takes for you to get turned off?"

Suzanne sighed. "He's from Germany, Carol. A visiting professor. I would imagine after a few stints of teaching here, he'll go back to his country. Why don't you give this ad thing a chance?"

"How much does it cost?" I asked again.

"The ad is free. The money is made when people call the 900 number to respond or when you call the 900 number to retrieve your responses. That's a dollar seventy-nine a minute."

I winced. I was still adjusting to running a house on a single income. "I can't afford this."

"I figure that I'll have about a hundred-dollar phone bill, but think of the money you'll save now that you don't have to call your mom long distance."

I let pass Suzanne's assumption that either my mom or I were given to chatting on the phone.

My gaze floated back to the ads. They were, at minimum, entertaining to read. "Listen to this one, Suzanne. No big hair, New Agers, tie-dye or Republicans."

Suzanne chuckled. "Call him."

"I have big hair."

"Your hair is gorgeous."

It was certainly more distinctive than my neck.

The fog was collecting into visibility. I moved my chair directly under the outdoor heater. A concert of plastic scraping concrete erupted on the crowded patio as other people shifted their chairs. The moment reminded me of when Suzanne waved at the Roaring Camp Train and her action set off a chain of raised arms and fluttering fingers.

"I listen to what the guys have to say on their phone message," Suzanne said, "and if they sound strange, I simply don't call them. And even if I do call, I might decide that we don't have enough in common."

Suzanne chewed her fry with her front teeth. She reminded me of a rabbit. Make that a bunny. "Part of what I like about this process is that it helps me to clarify what I *do* want."

"And what is that, Suzanne?"

"Adventure. Someone different. Someone who pulls me away from my content little Santa Cruz life. It's great here, but I do the same thing day after day. Even with the magnificence and abundance, I experience a sort of sensory deprivation."

I played with a French fry, painting a red heart on my napkin. I knew exactly what Suzanne meant. Life in Santa Cruz was easy, so it was easy to become complaisant.

"Hey, there's Beverly." Suzanne pointed with her chin toward the doorway into the bar. Beverly Levandowsky, the cook in our Employees Dining Room, was a bigger, bustier, and brassier version of Suzanne. The chefs at Archibald's fantasized about her so much that they forgot to salt their sauces. Unless a little saliva fell into the pot. And that was when she was dressed in our work uniform of white smock and hounds-tooth pants. At this moment she wore tight black short shorts and a clingy white tank top. She arched back against the stucco wall of the building and chewed on a straw as she chatted with a lean man dressed in black leather pants and a leather vest. A graying braid dangled down his back.

Beverly had been hired because she was Suzanne's cousin. That was back when our big, pudgy kitchen manager Eldon still had a hopeless crush on Suzanne, before she'd warded him off with a fictitious story regarding a case of herpes.

People in the kitchen didn't resent Beverly's lack of cooking experience. The Employees Dining Room was a place to learn how to operate a steam table and how to utilize leftovers. We resented the nepotism, but only because it wasn't our cousin who got the job.

Suzanne waved to Beverly.

Beverly said something to the man, who frowned at us and then assumed a waiting stance against the wall. She wove through the tables towards us. Her summer toenails, painted vermilion, peeked from the straps of her black sandals. She had an anklet tattoo and legs like Marilyn Monroe. Behind her, heads turned like the wake of a boat.

"Hey, kiddo," she greeted Suzanne. Beverly removed the straw from her mouth and leaned down to give Suzanne a peck on the cheek, enveloping both of us in a cloud of musky perfume. "Hi ya, Carol."

Her fingernails sported the same vibrant red as her toenails. She wore a sapphire ring the size of a marble, drove a red Miata, and lived in a condo by the harbor. All the kitchen staff speculated about where she got the cash. It certainly didn't come from her salary. Since there was no hint of an ex-husband or money in the family, most of us figured she had a sugar daddy.

"You two look stunning," Beverly gushed. "Carol, I've never seen you in anything but your uniform. Girl, you should flaunt that body more often."

Donning my Lycra shorts and a black tank top that said Spikettes across the front, the name of my former volleyball team, I'd had no thought of flaunting my body. But I didn't feel offended. Beverly's warm effervescence made a person feel good regardless of what she was saying.

"I can't stay," she bubbled. "I'm tied up." She said this salaciously, winking at both of us, and glancing back at the guy waiting for her. "Nice seein' you, Carol."

Her departure reminded me of a vacuum sealer, taking all the air with her, flattening everything left behind.

Suzanne's Volkswagen putted down Seventh Avenue, past the boat businesses that served the Santa Cruz Yacht Harbor. Alternative music blasted from the cassette player.

I reached over, and twisted down the volume. "Let me see if I got this right. You want to send your cousin Beverly on a date with one of the guys who called in response to your ad?"

"Yup."

"Why?"

"You don't think it's a good idea?" she asked.

"No. I don't."

"Why not?"

I wasn't sure. "Because the guy thinks it's you."

"This guy doesn't know me from Eve." Suzanne turned onto Soquel Drive and headed down the busy thoroughfare. This section of the road gave the illusion of country, dropping off on the right into a riparian corridor. "And he said stuff on his message that made me think he'd be Beverly's type."

"Like what?"

"This is confidential." Her eyes shot me a concerned glance.

"Of course." I was nothing if not discreet.

"Sorry." She drove a moment, turned off the music, and collected her thoughts. "The guy—Mike—said he likes to experiment, take risks."

"Experiment. What do you mean *experiment*?"

"Calm down, Carol."

"What do these guys *say* when they call, anyway?" My voice pitched with curiosity and concern. I liked Suzanne. I didn't want her on a date with someone into taking risks.

"Not *these guys*, Carol. One guy. Mike. To me, he seemed presumptuous to even be discussing sex, but I thought he'd be perfect for Beverly. He was frank about wanting an adventurous sexual partner, and he listed what he meant."

"And what *did* he mean?"

Suzanne gave a chest-heaving sigh that strained the straps of her sundress. "Stuff Bev likes."

"What exactly is that?"

"You call me persistent." Suzanne turned into my neighborhood. She was either blushing or glowing in the rose of the sunset.

I waited her out.

"Bondage, for starters. This guy Mike must have gotten the wrong idea from the *tie-the-knot* part of the ad."

"Beverly likes bondage?" I forced my voice to stay calm, hoping that Suzanne would tell me more.

She made another turn into my cul-de-sac and stopped. Lola sprang through the Mexican wild roses and mewled piteously at the passenger door of the yellow Volkswagen. Her tail had been shot off in my last escapade, and even though Lola didn't seem to notice she had only a stump, I felt pangs of guilt every time the beautiful tortie greeted me unable to lift and quiver her tail.

"Bev's not into sadomasochism, just play."

"Leather and whips?" I couldn't contain my prurient curiosity.

"Not a big whip." Suzanne shifted the car to neutral and removed her sandaled foot from the clutch. "A quirt."

"A *quirt*? What the hell is a *quirt*?" I didn't get out in spite of Lola waiting outside the door. I was a bad mother. It was a good thing I'd confined myself to one belligerent cat.

"A little riding crop," Suzanne explained, unlatching my seatbelt.

"So she likes to horse around?"

Suzanne groaned, reached across my lap and pulled the door handle.

"Wait. I don't want to go, Suzanne. My house is so cold and lonely and gloomy and desolate and did I say lonely?"

"You have Lola." At the sound of the door release, the cat's cries had increased to demonic wails.

"She's not as good as you and stories of quirts and bondage. I want to know more."

"Thanks a lot, but this is why you need to make that call, Carol."

"What if he's someone like Mike?"

"You might like it."

"Do you?" I pulled the door back shut.

"This is the last time I'm taking you for a beer, Carol."

She turned off the engine, a good sign.

"You're being evasive. That shifts my suspicious, detective mind into overdrive."

"Let's put it this way, Carol. I have nothing against light bondage. If both parties are interested, it can be fun, although, for me, personally, it's better as a fantasy. No, Mike sounds more like Beverly's type, and besides, I'm interested in Hamad."

"Hamad! A Muslim?" I melodramatically clutched handfuls of my wiry hair.

"Hamad Marzouk."

"Really?"

"Don't tell me you're racist as well as a prude."

"Come on. Of course I'm a prude. I've been having married sex for the last umpteen years, and is it wrong to get upset about a people who believe in clitoridectomies?"

"Some Muslims believe in clitoridectomies."

"Where's this Hamad from?"

"Kuwait."

"Oh, Kuwait. Such a liberated place."

"Most *Americans* think we liberated it, yes," she said sardonically.

"A man can legally kill his wife there. All he has to do is claim she was unfaithful." Lola's cries pierced the car, as though she were one of the oppressed women of the world. Perhaps she was, since I wouldn't allow her to become contentedly obese.

"Not all Kuwaitis are like that." Suzanne straightened in the black bucket seat. "As a matter of fact, Hamad's an antiroyalist."

"Bondage, a renegade Muslim . . . ."

Suzanne shoved gently on my shoulder. "I have to go. I have a date with Hamad."

"You're going to abandon me to this lonely, bleak, gloomy, desolate . . . ."

"Don't forget 'cold,'" Suzanne said as she pushed open my door.

"Cold, lonesome . . ." I continued as I climbed out. Lola butted my leg. Overhead, the palm swished against the twilight sky. ". . . desolate," I mouthed through the closed window as Suzanne waved a golden hand and started the car.

I turned toward the tiny, pinkish-white stucco house, welcoming as a Gothic church.

# CHAPTER 3

Two days later, I sat in the Employees' Dining Room drinking lemonade and watching Beverly. I tried to focus on the listing agreement for the house that Chad and I had tentatively completed the night before. I had seller's remorse and we hadn't even listed yet. Pondering Beverly's sexuality was more compelling than wallowing in the morass of fear the listing agreement inspired.

The only other people in the room were Rigoberto, the new dishwasher, and José, a new back-line chef. They huddled over large glasses of ice water, chatting quietly in Spanish, glancing furtively at Beverly, bumping shoulders, and occasionally laughing.

"You okay, honey?" Beverly dropped into a chair at my table. Now that I'd seen her exposed legs and arms, she'd never look the same in her uniform.

"Do you know anything about real estate?"

"I know that the first three things you consider are location, location and location."

"I'm selling. I think."

Her warm eyes regarded me. I stomped out thoughts of Beverly dressed in black leather and wielding a whip. Or rather, a quirt.

"Chad let me stay in our house, but we're selling it to split the equity," I said. "But I might take the plunge and cash in my savings to buy him out. Not that I even have enough." Not to mention I'd have nothing to fall back on if I wanted to get started as a private investigator. The move to buy the house would lock me into my job at Archibald's.

"That kind of decision is much scarier than a little spanking."

My face blazed hot with embarrassment.

"Look," she said, "Suzanne is a honeypot, but she's piss poor at keeping secrets. And you," she laughed out loud, "let me put it this way. Don't play poker."

"Well I'm not the type to blab." I checked the wall clock. Our kitchen manager timed employees' breaks.

Beverly shrugged as though indifferent. "I don't care if you talk. It could be good advertising. Just don't get too curious. Some of the people in my world are what you might call unsavory characters." She rose from the chair and meandered toward the two workers who gawked as she approached. "Cómo están, amigos?" she greeted them.

"Good. Good," José said, practically falling out of his chair while Rigoberto simply stared.

Those *unsavory characters* leapt to mind when Beverly made front-page news two weeks later.

Suzanne unfolded the newspaper onto my plastic patio table, which after the divorce, had moved into the house as an essential piece of furniture. My place was gloomy enough to match Suzanne's expression. Fog curled outside the windows, socking in even my banana-belt neighborhood.

The front-page photo showed splayed legs, short skirt hitched high, and the contents of a woman's purse strewn through the weeds.

It was our local journalism at its finest. I felt angry at the invasion of privacy, even though the woman was dead. *Dead!* I was having trouble grasping the idea the photo was of Beverly. An ice pick drove up through my stomach.

Paralyzed on one of my folding white plastic chairs, I read the article while Suzanne stood, gripping the edge of the table. Her face was ashen.

The article used the word grisly twice. Beverly had been strangled and the body dumped on the levee of the San Lorenzo River, behind the thrift shops on Front Street. Robbery had "not been ruled out as a motive," the police chief had been quoted. It was not clear whether there'd been any sexual assault.

"How could that be *not clear?*"

"I don't know." In faded jeans, a baggy, cream-colored sweater, and no makeup, Suzanne looked about .5 below her usual ten.

I patted a chair for her to sit, but the chairs were less than inviting in the best of circumstances. She remained standing.

"There's going to be an autopsy and I'm sure I can give you all the sordid details."

Possibly, I thought. The information could be withheld as a way to eliminate false confessions or to confirm the murderer. "Even with this photo," I murmured, "it's hard to believe that Beverly's dead." I shook my head.

In the newspaper a sidebar on the increasing problem of the homeless, some of whom lived under the San Lorenzo River bridges, added further implications.

"What bullshit," Suzanne stabbed at the paper with a chipped nail. "I told the police it was that Mike. It wasn't any homeless person."

"Did you talk to Detective Carman or Detective Peters?" After sticking my nose into two murders, I'd become acquainted with the local homicide detectives.

Suzanne wiped a bloated cheek with the back of her hand, a reflex after a day of nearly continuous crying. "I'm not sure. Detective Carman was one of them, I think. I have their cards at home." Suzanne was more coherent than she'd been yesterday.

At work everyone had been buzzing about Beverly not showing up and speculating on possible reasons. Suzanne had fallen into a silent funk, her hands shaking when she tried to dice carrots. Then her mom had called her and she'd left the kitchen. When we'd learned the reason, we clammed up. Even Eldon, who could manage the kitchen after singeing his eyelashes with a misjudged bananas flambé, fell into a stupor, shocked, that a second person from our kitchen had been murdered.

None of us knew Beverly well enough to share Suzanne's anguish, but having anyone you know die in an untimely, dramatic way unnerved a person. Between ladling three-onion soup and arranging cheese twists in a basket, we took turns giving each other hugs and pats.

Eldon declared the Employees Dining Room closed for the day and transferred himself from Beverly's job to Suzanne's position as *garde manger*.

In the foggy gloom of my house, I hunched over the newspaper article, re-reading slowly and carefully, since the first time I hadn't been able to concentrate. I offered Suzanne tea, but she shook her head. "I can barely keep anything down." She hovered above me like a mournful ghost.

The body had been discovered and reported only hours after Beverly's death by two people on an early morning bike ride.

*"At first we didn't think anything,"* the man, David Shapiro, was quoted. *"Just another homeless person sleeping in the brush. But there was something about the way she was laying and her clothes that didn't fit that idea."*

He referred to his biking partner as a "friend," although an astute reader would wonder what kind of female *friend* would be available for a seven a.m. bike ride.

I patted the plastic chair beside me again, but Suzanne shook her head and chewed the edge of her thumb.

I refocused on the article. David Shapiro's friend, Regina Smith, seemed reticent to talk about the discovery. She said it was "horrible," and that David persuaded her to look, but she was frightened.

"I want to hire you," Suzanne said.

I glanced up into her anguished face. My fingers tingled

with excitement. My stomach executed somersaults. I was one sick puppy. Why was I wired this way? I wanted to get down in the weeds, to snoop around and track down the truth, and it had only a little to do with avenging Beverly's death. It had more to do with the abstract notion of justice and the thrill of it all.

I felt like a dog straining at a leash, barely able to obey my master, my conscience. "I'm not officially a private investigator, yet. I haven't even taken the exam." The written exam was nothing compared to the required six thousand hours of supervised training.

"You solved two murders without being an investigator at all."

I reached up and latched on to Suzanne's thin, cold hand. My touch opened a floodgate of tears. I squeezed her hand as she fought for control.

Besides acting out of guilt that she may have directed Beverly to her killer, Suzanne might be tossing her poor buddy—moi—a bone. Everyone at work knew that I wanted to buy out Chad's interest in the house but didn't quite have the money. Given half a chance, they would have devised a Cook Off fundraiser for me.

My stubborn pride balked at any hint of charity. But most likely early clients would be friends or friends of friends. And they were grown-up people who could choose to spend their money as they wished. As Suzanne's tears subsided, I said, "It costs a lot to hire a private investigator."

She pulled away her hand. "I don't care," she said flatly. "I feel responsible for what happened. If I hadn't lined her up with that—Mike—maybe she'd be alive."

"Maybe."

Suzanne rolled her eyes. "Who else could it be, Carol?" She sounded almost snotty. "I'd talked to Beverly about this guy maybe ten days ago, but that very day," she slapped at the newspaper for emphasis, "the very day she said she was going to call him, she was murdered." Suzanne rooted around in the pocket of her jeans and poked a slip of paper toward me. "Here's the guy's phone number."

It struck me as extremely unlikely that a murderer had given out his real phone number. "This seems so easy and straight forward. Why not just let the police handle it?"

"Do you want this job or not?"

"I'm dying to take it, but you're my friend and I want you to know what you're getting into. This could be solved by the police tomorrow and you'd be out of a retainer."

"Not likely," she snorted.

"Or, it might be way more complicated than either of us imagined. We could get into thousands of dollars."

"Look, Carol, I've been saving for a big trip to Costa Rica, so I have a couple of thousand set aside for fun. But how am I going to soak up the sun in Playa Hermosa with this over my head? I'll never feel right if I don't do something."

I accepted the phone number and her check.

# CHAPTER 4

Now I felt guilty. This was too easy. I had the day off and a huge photo of the crime scene. I knew the victim's identity and had a close relationship with the victim's cousin. Information spread before me that the police had to work to gather.

I was heading toward the address of David Shapiro. I hadn't even run a search on the computer to find his address. It had been listed conveniently in the phone book. In the pocket of my jeans I could feel the crisp check for five hundred dollars. Life would have been grand if this case hadn't come from Beverly's death.

The first time I'd seen Beverly had been in the Employees Dining Room on her first day of work. Instead of floundering in self-absorbed insecurity like most new employees, she enthusiastically greeted everyone who entered. "Hi. How ya doing?" If there were any feature for which I envied her, it wasn't her legs or breasts, but her outgoing, generous personality, the ease with which she extended herself.

My brother Donald had embodied the same personality. It seemed like he'd inherited all the Latino genes—the dark good looks and warmth—while I was strictly white bread. If my mother were another woman, I would have suspected that Donald and I had different fathers.

I remembered Donald handing me a long-sleeved black jersey he'd won in a ten-kilometer race. He'd said, "This is for you because you're my sister and I love you." We weren't a family that went around saying, "I love you." I'd worn that shirt until the graphics had faded into oblivion and holes pocked the seams. It was now retired to the bottom drawer of my dresser.

I shook my head so that I could drive. The memory of Donald frequently ambushed me like this. My fingertips on the steering wheel felt hollow.

Donald and I had undulated in and out of closeness. We'd played together as children until he had started school. This had caused a huge rift for two years until I started school, too. Then we were close again, with Donald acting as a directory of information about teachers and who to avoid on the playground. But the older-brother-guide period was followed by an epoch of estrangement with a sign on his bedroom door that said, "No Girls Allowed, Expecially Tom Girls." Even when Donald decided girls made good friends, that didn't include little sisters. But finally, when he was a senior, pushing toward maturity, and I was a sophomore, our social lives started to overlap, and a tentative friendship developed that continued to grow up to the moment of his death.

I swallowed hard at the memory as I entered the unincorporated Live Oak area to the south of Santa Cruz. I'd heard Live Oak described as a cross between Oklahoma and Hawaii, a funky combination of rural redneck and surfer cultures, both endangered by rampant development.

To distract myself from memories of Donald, I reviewed my schedule for the day. It was a Friday, so normal people would be at work. But, if I had any luck, I'd interview David Shapiro. He had been first on the scene of the crime and was therefore a possible suspect. After that, I'd deposit the check, visit my mom, and time permitting, pay a visit to Regina Smith, David Shapiro's companion. By then, the police probably would have arrested a suspect.

David's brown ranch-style house ran along a short street that dead-ended into an elementary school. I pulled my Karmann Ghia to the curb. Everything about the house screamed bachelor—from the rap music blaring from behind the garage door to the crab grass lawn. Nothing dainty adorned the house—no flowers in pots, no ceramic house numbers, no wind chimes or bird feeders. The living room drapes were closed. I could imagine a killer living here. Except for the blasting volume of the music.

A white Cabriolet convertible and a white Ford Escort station wagon filled the short driveway in front of the garage. They both seemed sleek compared to my rust red rattrap.

Stepping over a bottle of bicycle-chain lubricant and an oily rag on the porch, I pressed the doorbell, wondering if there was any chance it could be heard over the music. I waited. And waited. I pressed it again. Waited. Pressed it several times in a row. Nothing.

I walked over to the garage door and banged on it. Something fell. Whether imagined or real, I sensed a stunned silence under the pulsing music. The loud whir of an electric-garage-door opener made me jump back against the Escort.

"Hello," said the guy who occupied the open doorway. Any guy under my height—five foot eight—I considered short. This guy would have been staring levelly into my eyeballs except that his dark eyes were brazenly and appreciatively scanning me from my long hair to my black Converse high-tops in a way that I found obnoxious and appealing. I was pinned against the hood of the Escort.

Behind the man sat a young woman on a makeshift stage surrounded by halogen lights. She was sheathed in a pink terry robe that looked hastily gathered over a naked body. "I thought you were my neighbor coming to complain about the music," David Shapiro yelled over the rap. "He's in the Captain and Teneille fan club." Neither he nor the girl seemed at all nonplused by my intrusion. As a matter of fact, the girl yawned.

"I'm Carol Sabala."

David shouted his name over the music and gave me a firm handshake. He wore a white tee shirt advertising Garuda Airlines, baggy tan shorts and high top athletic shoes. "Let's call it a day, Annie," he called to the girl as he strode back into the garage. He handed her a twenty. Probably a fair estimate of her age.

Annie tweezered the bill with false fingernails, came down the two steps from the sheepskin rug on the stage, and hung the robe on one of the lamp poles. She had long, long legs, light pubic hair waxed into a tiny swatch, a flat belly, perky breasts with pink nipples, all wrapped in the nubile skin of youth. I felt myself sinking into my former funk. The garage door gaped open, but Annie didn't seem to care.

She stepped into black thong underwear. David Shapiro stared at her taut buns.

"Same time tomorrow, David?" she shouted at him over the lyrics about screams of a mother and dead n*****s in a gutter and other loveliness.

"No. We'll take the weekend off," he yelled back.

She pulled on a green sweatshirt. "Remember I have my Cabrillo classes on Tuesday and Thursday and my UCSC class on Wednesday."

They worked out the time of the next shoot in quick bursts of language as she finished dressing in baggy shorts to her knees and black shoes with chunky, platform heels. From a garage counter covered with a messy array of tools, she scooped up a small stack of jewelry.

In the pounding music, the rapper asked what good it all was when you were six feet under.

*Good question.*

Annie fluttered a handful of acrylic pink nails at David, mouthed "Nice to meet you" to me, and might have skipped to her white Cabriolet, blond hair bouncing, if her shoes hadn't weighed ten pounds.

David turned off the intense lights. We were alone. The front of the garage looked out into a parking lot for the school.

Behind the stage, a huge roll of blue paper had been pulled down to create a backdrop. The stage itself held a variety of props from a red velvet pillow to a black leather vest.

David beckoned me through the back door of the garage,

to the deck, and through the sliding glass door into his dining room. I followed cautiously, my self-defense mechanisms on high alert. Flesh to bone and bone to flesh, I reminded myself.

He went to a cart of high-tech stereo equipment and lowered the music, then quickly went about the dining room and living room turning on track lights. He wanted me to be impressed by the photography on the wall, and I was.

"Pretty cutting edge, don't you think?"

I nodded.

He smiled. "I'm in Open Studios. Do you ever take the tour?"

I shook my head. I'd heard of the countywide event and had seen the signs, but I'd never traveled around looking at the local artists' work.

His photography was mostly of people—a man from New Guinea wearing a penis gourd, a beautiful Vietnamese girl with black fingernails and gnarled hands from working with dyes, a street urchin in Nepal, his knees drawn up inside his ragged tee shirt. A burning corpse on a pyre. A pig's throat being slaughtered in a ritual ceremony. The photography was completely different from what he'd been concocting in the garage.

As if he could read my mind, he said, "The work with Annie is bread and butter."

"What about Annie?"

"Oh she is superbly fine, but I like my women to know Watergate is not like Water World."

He'd misinterpreted my question, but David Shapiro appealed to me. Under my wariness, sexual energy bubbled.

His dark eyes were alive with mischief. I needed to get down to business before I became distracted.

"I'm a private detective."

"Is this visit because of my neighbors or because of the dead woman?"

"The dead woman."

He seemed relieved. "My neighbors think I'm Satan." He

strolled into his kitchen, a large room undermined by dark wood, brown linoleum, and Seventies harvest gold appliances. It, too, had become a gallery for his photographs.

"Your photography is really good," I said, looking at a picture of a toothless woman holding out a handful of betel nuts. "It's amazing that all these people let you take their pictures."

"I never photograph an unwilling subject." He grinned. "Sometimes a little money exchanged hands."

Whether money had sealed the deal or not, David Shapiro clearly possessed a charm that could elicit a smile from an ancient Ecuadorian Indian woman or from a small Jamaican boy. But the photos were disturbing, too. Combine the violence of the ritual pig slaughter with the sex in the garage and one could come up with a snuff film. "You've traveled the world."

He beamed, unabashedly proud of himself. "Would you like some different music?" He moved back to the stereo system in the dining room.

"Any Captain and Teneille?"

He smiled at me. Big. Fresh. Full of straight teeth. Ted Bundy was quite handsome, I reminded myself.

"No," he said, "but believe it or not, I do have Chopin."

"Maybe no music would be best since I'm here to work."

"Work is overrated."

"Except this is my first investigation, and it's what I've always wanted to do."

"I'm an investigator, too."

*Investigator?* The paper hadn't mentioned that detail. As usual, my face betrayed me and revealed my incredulity. I can stare down a basilisk, but as Beverly had noted, my facial expressions are pitifully obvious. "I can read you like a book," my mom said.

"My day job," he explained. "Part-time for the State of California."

"What do you investigate?"

"Violations in care facilities. Group homes. Homes for the

disabled. For example, some immigrant fresh off the boat and indentured to his money-grubbing relatives decides his pay should include some action with a cute little retard. Stuff like that."

David Shapiro offended and attracted me at the same time. His political incorrectness spoke right to my primal love of bad boys.

The guy kept inspecting me. "You're an interesting woman, Carol Sabala."

I itched with the need to get this interview back on a professional plane. I should be treating David Shapiro like a potential suspect, the killer returning to the scene of the crime, one of Beverly's *unsavory characters.* "Let's talk about Beverly Levandowsky."

"Okay. Although between the detectives and the reporters, I'm kinda talked out on the subject."

He led me across the brown shag carpet of the living room to the sunny front steps. "Wanna beer?"

I shook my head. I wanted David Shapiro to stop acting like I was a potential date and to start acting like I was a detective. I had to reassess my approach, become more intent, maybe not wear my Converse and jeans, maybe insist on a formal setting like the dining room table.

"Cookies? They're from Pacific Cookie Company?"

I nodded even though after years of baking, I'd become invulnerable to the appeal of cookies. As David went into the house, I pictured myself in a suit. If I couldn't wear my Converse and jeans, my newfound career would lose some of its appeal. One of the things I disliked about my current job was the uniform—chef's smock, hounds-tooth pants, and chef's hat. Besides, I rationalized, people were more likely to divulge information if they felt comfortable with me, and they were more likely to be comfortable with me if I were dressed informally.

David returned with two paper napkins and a plastic bag

full of cookies. He toed aside the bike oil and rag and sat, leaning on a supporting post of the stoop. I sat on the step. He exuded the energy of a young man. About fourteen. But in the sun I saw the fine wrinkles at the base of his ears and in the corners of his eyes.

"You saw the paper," he asserted. "That photo belongs on the shelf by the *Chopper* magazines."

"Exactly," I said, delighted. "Next to *True Detective*."

He nodded vigorously, smacking on a cookie.

"So you were out for a bike ride at what six, seven o'clock with Regina Smith?"

"A co-worker. We were mountain biking. I have an ultra cool aluminum-frame Trek. Do you ride?"

"I need to stay on task, Mr. Shapiro." The sun was shining. Finches tweeted in the sycamore in front of his house.

"Do you have a bike?"

"An old three speed."

"Let's go for a ride."

"Right now?"

He nodded.

"I can't. I have work to do."

"Work is for sissies."

I smiled. "Maybe we can ride after I finish my investigation."

"I guess, then, that I better share with you a couple of interesting morsels."

# CHAPTER 5

I found a parking spot across from the Hinds House and trudged toward the obligatory meeting with my mom. I tried to think of what might be reasonable boundaries for us. Once a week get-togethers? Since we were both in vulnerable states, me, recently divorced, and she, recently transplanted, it was hard to assess what would be right. I didn't plan to stay single and lonely forever, although I wasn't exactly doing anything about changing my plight. I beat back fleeting visions of Klaus Holthuis and David Shapiro, two physically very different men, who'd both sent my pulse racing. Maybe Suzanne was right. I'd gone too long without any sex action.

I mounted the broad, elegant steps of Hinds House and cranked the key in the door. A vision of David Shapiro was replaced with the sight of my mother. Today she was decked out in green shorts and a shirt with stripes of green, purple, blue and pale yellow. Over the shirt she wore a knitted green vest. Not a bad outfit. Rather dapper, even.

"Were you waiting at the door?" I said testily.

"Well bless your little heart. I think somebody woke up on the wrong side of the bed."

My mom had said "bless your little heart" since I was a child, so "little" was probably an affectionate holdover, but I was suspicious. Maybe she meant I had a small heart. I felt like I did. My mom's "wrong side of the bed" cliché rankled.

"Who else would be answering the bell on a work day?" she added. "The other folks are not retirees."

I guess that meant that I wouldn't be seeing Klaus. I

followed her into the parlor where she was in the process of
knitting a dark blue sweater. I sat beside her on the velour
couch. She resumed her knitting.

I wondered what my life would have been like if I'd had
a young mother. Compared to Suzanne's mother, my mom
seemed like a grandmother. She had been over thirty and established in her career when she'd met my dad, a good thing since
he'd run off and left her. That must have been humiliating for
someone like my mom who put so much stock in image. In a
small town like Ferndale, everyone must have gossiped about it.

I stared at the lacy sheers on the windows and wished
I could see through them. The needles clacked into the eerie
silence of the Victorian.

"So how's it going, Mom? How's that weird neighbor of
yours?"

She shushed me.

"I thought you said no one else was home."

"Not that I know of."

"Then why are you shushing me?"

"Walls have ears."

My patience was gone. If I stayed here in the straight-laced
Victorian parlor with her whacking needles and aphorisms, I'd
go nuts. "Would you like to go out for coffee?"

Her eyes lit. "Oh yes. I discovered an interesting little
coffee shop."

"What's it called?"

"Starbucks."

I rolled my eyes.


At Starbucks, after I got my mom settled at a table with
a mocha and a peanut butter cookie, she piped up, "I heard
about that girl getting murdered on the levee."

The tone was accusatory. Did my mom already suspect I
was involved in the case?

"You didn't tell me this town was so . . . "

She stared out the window at the young man sitting on the sidewalk, cardboard sign propped beside him: *Living on the street sucks. Please help. God bless.* A little bowl waited for change.

". . . strange."

I inwardly beat myself up. I'd never imagined my mom would up and move to Santa Cruz. I had smugly bragged to her about our great weather and beaches. If I'd been more alert to her plans, I would have told her that back in 1972 Santa Cruz had been dubbed "The Murder Capital of the World." Mass murderers John Lindley Frazier, Herbert Mullen and Edmond Kemper had all chosen victims from the area, and the Santa Cruz Mountains were still a popular place to dump bodies. But how could I have known that my mom would pull up her stakes in the rural Ferndale area and retire to Santa Cruz?

On the other hand, my mom hadn't said dangerous, she'd said strange. Purple hair and nipple rings might have been better talismans against her moving here.

I nursed a plain, small coffee. I liked things undiluted, especially the truth. "Strange like your housemate, Mom?"

She shot me a sharp glance.

"Tell me more about Klaus."

"He's German." She sipped her mocha. For her, Germans had never ceased being Nazis.

"You must have some details." I watched a tourist drop a quarter into the young man's bowl. Eldon frequently told the story of how he'd offered twenty-five dollars in exchange for yard work to a man with a Will-Work-for-Food sign. The man had told Eldon that he could make more standing at the freeway exit.

"Why do you always want the sordid details?" my mom sighed with exasperation. "You've always been like that, Carol, turning up rocks to find pill bugs and digging in the mud for salamanders."

This from a woman who'd probed people's mouths and

measured the pockets in their gums.

"I think he shaves more than his chin," my mom offered.

"What? Like what? How would you know that?"

"We share a bathroom." My mom smugly sipped her drink. "Men are the same way about cleaning up hairs as they are about putting down the toilet seat."

"How do you know the hairs aren't from his face?"

"They're in the bathtub. They're dark."

I could think of explanations for the hair besides Klaus shaving nether parts of his body, but I decided not to pursue the argument. Nor did I offer that a lot of people might appreciate a tidy bush.

As it turned out, my mom didn't know much more about Klaus than Suzanne had learned in twenty minutes. Klaus had moved to Santa Cruz from some other university town in the states. He was a visiting professor in foreign language.

"And what makes you think he's sexually weird?"

My mom pursed her lips as though to shush me, but didn't because it would have called attention to us. In spite of the clothes she wore, my mom did not like to be the center of attention. At least anything she might have construed as negative attention. She looked around the small but busy store, then put her grizzled head next to mine. "He's on the same floor as I am."

"Yes."

"I saw him on our landing with a young girl, must have been a student."

"Yes."

"She was making a cup of tea."

"Yes."

"I walked out of my room. He'd just opened his briefcase on the counter. Right on top of his papers, he had a pair of handcuffs."

I waited. But there was no more.

"That's it?"

"What kind of professor has handcuffs in his briefcase?"

"Maybe he cuffs his briefcase to a chair so no one can steal it."

She shook her head. "These were black leather with furry linings."

"So you think he wanted the girl to see these cuffs. Like some kind of suggestion?"

I imagined myself naked facing a white wall, my hands above me in cuffs. Klaus behind me, fully dressed. He pressed against me, cupped my breasts, and in his accented voice whispered in my ear, "I . . . ."

". . . know he was making a suggestion," my mom was saying, her withered cheeks blushing.

"How?"

She wiggled on her chair. "Because of what I overheard through my transom window."

Ah hah! I knew that my snoopy genes had come from somewhere. The only difference between my mom's snooping and mine was that I didn't pretend to be proper and respectful of other's privacy. "So what did you hear, Mom?"

"They were discussing in this very intellectual way the role fantasy plays in a rich . . . sex life."

"And you decided you had to walk out and see what was going on?"

She nodded. "After all, this man just moved here and now a woman has been murdered."

"Mom, you just moved here, too."

This warranted a scathing look.

"If you'd like," I said in my most ameliorating voice, "I could do a background check on this guy." That was, after all, the typical kind of work for a private investigator. Not that I didn't have an ulterior motive or two.

She nodded. "Usually I like to mind my own business. I don't like to pry into people's . . . private lives, but he is living right next door to me."

"Lots of people would be concerned."

Licking the end of her finger, my mom dabbed up cookie crumbs. "What does a service like this cost?"

I shook my head.

"How are you going to make a living if you don't charge people?" She pulled her lips into a disgusted line.

"You're not *people*, you're my mother."

"You need every penny you can get to buy that house."

My mother's bluntness cut to the heart of the matter. I loved the way she dashed away bullshit, but it also made me fearful and uncomfortable, a large part of the reason I didn't want her so close. As strongly as I pursued the elusive truth, I preferred false hope to no hope.

I had talked Chad out of listing the house and into giving me one month to come up with a way to buy him out. If I could swing it, he'd quit claim his right to the property and allow me to continue payment on the mortgage for which we'd qualified together. A generous agreement on his part. I could manage the mortgage part. If worse came to worse, I'd get a housemate. One thing was for sure, though. I would never qualify for a new mortgage by myself. But how I'd scrape together the lump sum to buy Chad out, was, as my mother had so eloquently pointed out, problematic.

Faced with my stubbornness, my mom sighed, compressed her lips again, and stared at the panhandler on the sidewalk. "Everything is worth what its purchaser will pay for it," she said, resorting to a maxim. "If you charge nothing, you are saying your services are worth nothing."

"Okay, mom," I said exasperated, "how about ten thousand dollars for the background check?"

She sipped her mocha. "Okay. Ten thousand dollars."

The offer was ridiculous. I called her bluff. "I could find out a lot more, Mom, if I had this guy's social security number. Is there anything in the Hinds House that might give you access to that?"

"Of course not." She stiffened. The idea! But as she chewed the last of her cookie, her funk of indignation dissipated. "I might be able to find out."

She didn't retract her offer. The woman was as stubborn as I was, and also as snoopy. I glowed with smug satisfaction. As my mom might say, "The acorn never falls far from the tree."

# CHAPTER 6

I drove toward Regina Smith's house; she'd been with David Shapiro when he'd discovered the body.

My mind was in a hubbub. It refused to focus on the case, and kept escaping to thoughts about my life. My sex life with Chad had been so *standard*. Neither of us had challenged the other's idea of normal. I'd thought everything was fine, but now I wondered how it might be to have something a little spicier.

Provided I could ever find a partner. Not so easy with my schedule. Early to bed and up by four a.m. Eldon had recently approached me about the idea of hiring a second baker. I worked five days a week and various people in the kitchen filled the spot of baker on my two days off. Eldon thought the quality of Archibald's demanded a second *real* baker. However, nobody wanted the position for only two days a week.

In short, Eldon wanted to reduce my job to four days and to hire another person for three days, creating two part-time employees. Archibald's wouldn't have to pay the new employee benefits, and might try to wiggle out of paying mine.

We had no union. I didn't know what I'd do if I was simply scheduled for four days a week. I could barely live on what I made working five days a week. Such a change couldn't hit at a worse time, when I'd just talked Chad out of listing the house, and into negotiating a deal with me. On the other hand, maybe it was a good time for Eldon to cut my hours. One door closing, another opening. Maybe I was meant to receive this extra push into the world of investigating. And then there was my mom's ridiculous employment offer, nothing more than a thin front to help me out.

When I exited the freeway to Soquel Avenue, I paid attention to the directions David Shapiro had given me to Regina Smith's house. Part of the chaos in my brain sprang from the information he'd shared. Information he had not shared with the police. Not confiding in the police was suspicious, but if I'd done what David had, I wouldn't have confided in the police either, because what he'd done was not kosher.

I turned at the urban sprawl of Staples on the corner of 17th Avenue. Across the freeway squatted Circuit City and Toys 'R Us. Their landscaping looked like something from a pygmy forest and their cement walls bounced the traffic roar back to the residential community on the other side of the freeway. The neighborhood spoke to me—Andy of Mayberry infrastructure, unready for the onslaught of the modern world.

At Brommer Street I turned left and then made another right heading back toward the ocean. Regina Smith lived in a faded yellow wooden house. She answered the door as soon as the bell rang, said hello in a neutral voice, and sized me up with lovely hazel eyes as I sized her up with my own aquamarine portals to the soul.

Regina held herself like a dancer, her spine straight and lifted out of her hips. Old blue jeans that rode low revealed a flat stomach and belly button ring. Her breasts were liberated under her crop-top tee shirt. She didn't wear make-up and didn't need it.

I introduced myself and gave her the short version of how I'd come to be involved in the investigation.

She tucked half of her boring bob behind an ear. She didn't need a fancy cut; her hair was thick and black. "So you met David?" She smirked, and did another candid assessment of my body.

"Yes." I was swimming in an emotional morass. Regina seemed too young to be interested in David, to be anything other than what he had explained to me. On her bare feet, her toenails glowed electric blue.

"Let's talk out here." She sat on the red concrete steps. "I have housemates."

I lowered myself beside her, feeling divorced and old, but not ready for recycling. "So I understand you and David are co-workers?"

Regina barked like a seal, and then laughed. "He wishes."

I felt annoyed. My mom said that I got the red highlights in my hair and the impatience that went with them from her Grandpa Turner, who may or may not have killed his wife.

"My mom is a state licensee," Regina said. "She runs a care facility for the elderly and I work for her. I met David through our state inspector, but you'd have to stretch quite a ways to say David and I are co-workers."

"Maybe he meant the modeling."

She blushed slightly and wrinkled her nose. "Yeah, maybe." Her embarrassment seemed to stem from being caught out rather than from modesty. Their "professional" relationship was one of the tidbits David had shared with me. I wanted to know about her and David and modeling, but none of that was relevant to the case, unless modeling figured into the killer's modus operandi. I shook off the thought. "Tell me about discovering the body."

"It was creepy."

I waited. A Mexican sage grew beside the steps and bees droned around its stalks of purple blossoms. From each purple bud that had been kissed, a small white blossom erupted.

"We were riding really early," Regina whined. "It was foggy and spooky. It was like the setting for a horror film. I felt like David had set it up for us to discover the body."

I straightened. "What do you mean?"

"Well, you met him, right?"

"Yes." A hummingbird buzzed and swooped into the Mexican sage for a quick sip of nectar.

"Well, you must have gotten a hit of how insistent he can be."

"Yes."

"He was that way about the ride. 'Oh, you gotta go. It's so serene. You'll love it, Regina. It's the best time. There's no one else on the trail.' Et cetera."

"Okay," I said. "But since he is pushy about everything, being pushy about the ride would be normal behavior."

"I guess so," she said. "But since I've worked for him as a model, I know he's into creating a certain atmosphere and I just got a creepy feeling it was all orchestrated."

"Are you suggesting David Shapiro killed Beverly Levandowsky?"

"Well, no."

I tugged an earlobe. "Are you suggesting he knew the body was there?"

She threw her arms in the air, revealing all of her lovely tummy and most of her torso. "I don't know what I was suggesting, just that it was creepy." Agitated, her hands stretched out to shred a stalk of purple blossoms. "Then when we saw the body, he wanted to investigate."

"What did you want to do?"

"Ride away fast," she said, as though it were the most sane and natural response in the world.

Most people would probably agree with Regina. They'd want to flee, to pretend that Beverly was sleeping. Or if their suspicions gnawed at their consciences, they'd call the police from a safe distance. But the graphic, the violent, the weird pulled people like David and me, enticed us the way the sweet purple sage enticed the bees.

"And why did he have a camera in his bike bag?" Regina asked, cocking an eyebrow at me.

"Because he's a photographer?" My defense of David made me nervous. On the other hand, Regina seemed out to hang him.

She caught the note of sarcasm and her hazel eyes glinted.

"Not all photographers want to take pictures of a dead

body. That's pretty weird."

Since David had also shared this tidbit with me, I wasn't shocked. However, when he'd told me, he'd made his actions seem as normal as chocolate pudding. Of course one would take pictures. He was, after all, an investigator. Regina's rendition made the same actions seem as weird as cricket bread.

"And did you share any of this with the police?" I asked.

"Not really." She broke off another frond of sage.

"Why not?" The sun was beginning to slant away from us.

"Well, a lot of reasons."

I waited again. On my side of the steps gladiolus thrust toward the blue sky and were thickening toward blossoms. On the top bud, a thin ruff of yellow announced the imminent unfurling. As I'd hoped, Regina filled the silence. "First of all, like I told you, I thought what he did was creepy, but I didn't think he'd killed the woman."

I waited some more. On both sides of the walk, the scruffy grass needed to be mowed. It was particularly long around their mailbox, which was painted black and white like a cow.

"David also owed me a couple hundred dollars."

"Did he say he wouldn't pay you if you told?"

"No. But he did ask me not to tell."

"So you felt like he was extorting your silence?"

She shrugged, bent over, and picked at a blue toenail. "He is Leonard's good friend. That's my mom's licensing analyst. They bike together all the time. Licensing analysts can make it difficult for a facility if they want to."

"But David Shapiro is not a licensing analyst; he's an investigator. He never visits facilities unless there's a major problem. An investigation. Did you have some reason to believe he'd pressure his friend Leonard into making life difficult for your mom?"

She narrowed her eyes. "If something like that was going on, I wouldn't tell you."

# CHAPTER 7

That interview had been almost worthless. Regina's hostility toward David tainted everything she'd told me. But still I had to consider David Shapiro had found the body, photographed it, and asked, *maybe coerced*, the young woman to remain silent.

I drove on Portola Drive past the marshy Corcoran Lagoon and the KSCO building. I needed to feed Lola and myself. Except for the chocolate cookie with David Shapiro, I hadn't eaten since breakfast.

Dark blue-gray fog had gathered to the south above the ocean, and whispers of fog drifted into Live Oak.

I tried to figure out what I should do next. While David had taken photos of the crime scene, Regina had hung back. She hadn't told me anything about the crime scene that David hadn't already divulged. She seemed unaware of the final tidbit he'd given me—the strewn contents of Beverly's purse: tissues, an open wallet with no money, tampons, a pill bottle, make-up and an empty diaphragm case.

My stomach cried like a cat in heat and I considered making Lola wait while I dropped by Rosa's at the Yacht Harbor for a tostada gallinero. There was nothing in my refrigerator but condiments and wilting lettuce. I'd never been inspired to cook when there had been two of us, and I was less inspired now.

But I couldn't betray Lola.

At home, Lola pounced from the pink wild roses. Her eyes were round and green, her greeting shrill. "Yes, Lola, I, too, think this is an organized killer." I scratched under her chin, but she yowled louder. It was time for supper, damn it.

I checked the mail, a PG&E bill and a missing child card. Lola dashed before me through the door. I poured a cupful of kibbles into her dish and made the sudden decision that Lola had suffered enough. "No more diet for you, Lola."

I sat beside her on the tiled kitchen floor and stroked her dark fur highlighted with specks of gold and white. Her motor revved into full volume and the warm purr warded off some of the bleakness. The television and stereo had been Chad's and were gone. He'd taken the little maple table and caned chairs because I'd kept the metal-framed bed. The walls seemed blank and bare without the dreaded photo of his mom and the sexy Pamela Hanson poster of a woman putting on lipstick while her bare-chested lover watched. The man in the poster had had the same sultry sexiness as Chad.

Outside the sliding glass door, fog collected in my tiny backyard. The cold crept under the door and seeped up my spine. The house was too quiet. No Chad whistling. No one banging around in the other room, taking a shower, or listening to some inane television program. My stomach shrieked. I got up, checked the contents of my refrigerator, and selected a jar of black olives from the side pocket. I ate several, keeping the last pit in my mouth to gnaw with my teeth. An illusion of eating.

I went to the bedroom to check for phone messages. A red number one brightened my heart. "How about dinner?" David Shapiro's voice asked. "Thai, Mexican, Chinese, Italian, you name it, I know where the best is. Call me." He left his number.

I lay on my bed for a moment to take inventory. I needed to eat, didn't have anything in the house, and eating with David Shapiro seemed a lot more appealing than eating alone. What could I put on the other side of the scale? Professionalism? Girlish fear that I might seem too eager? They didn't even weigh in.

He could be a murderer. Ted Bundy was not only handsome, but much touted for his charm.

I looked about the room, the white walls and wood floors.

The house was tiny, no more than eight hundred square feet, but perfect for a single person. I had pinched pennies to stash away twenty thousand in a tax-shelter annuity and I could borrow the money from it interest free. But I'd still need a large loan to pay off Chad and I doubted I could qualify. I'd already have debt with the mortgage I'd be paying by myself.

The ring of the phone startled me. Thinking it might be David, I managed an upbeat greeting.

"You sound cheery," the voice said accusingly.

"Hi, Suzanne."

"What have you found out?"

"I don't think David Shapiro did it."

"David Shapiro? Who's th-? The guy who found Beverly? I never thought he did kill her." Suzanne's voice pitched toward hysteria. "Did you call Mike?"

I didn't answer.

"You know—*Mike?*" she said sarcastically, the guy who responded to my personal ad? The guy I lined up with Beverly? The guy who choked her to death?"

Suzanne was already having doubts about hiring me. She'd latched on to an idea and couldn't believe I hadn't followed up on it. She was suffering from the tyranny of the original idea, as most of us stubborn folk do.

"I haven't forgotten," I said calmly. "I will get on that." This would be the problem of investigating for friends. They had your home number. Suzanne felt entitled to a blow-by-blow account, and my guilt said she was entitled. The victim had been Beverly. Her cousin. As children, they'd played together in a sandbox.

"Are you eating?" Again the slightly annoyed tone like I wasn't supposed to eat while on the case.

"Just sucking on an olive pit."

"The police came to Archibald's today."

I was sorry I'd missed that. "What happened?"

"It was like when Jean was killed. They interviewed us.

Eldon was going nuts. He's trying to do Beverly's job and manage the kitchen, too, so filling in for the people they were interviewing pushed him over the edge. He actually used the word 'damn' with that Detective Carman."

*Poor Eldon.* "What did the police ask?"

"All the usual stuff. Was Beverly involved with anyone at work? Had any of us known of her plans for Wednesday night? Did any of us have any reason to kill her?" Suzanne sounded a little calmer. "So tell me about your day of investigating."

I walked with the phone to my study, one room that looked the same since Chad's departure, and used the time-honored technique of pulling out the palaver.

"I believe the killer is organized, rather than disorganized," I said, consulting my notes from my criminal justice class.

"What does that mean?" Suzanne asked.

"It means he's above-average intelligence, socially and sexually competent, and probably high in birth-order status. He may have a partner and most likely has a car in working condition. Although he planned this crime and is getting his jollies by following the news coverage, he probably wouldn't stick out in a crowd."

"I knew the paper was off base pointing a finger at the homeless."

"Well, there are a couple of bothersome details," I added. "For instance, an organized killer usually hides the body."

"Beverly was hidden in a way. Don't you think?"

"Sort of." Other elements of the crime didn't quite fit the profile of an organized killer. An organized killer usually went after a submissive victim, and Beverly struck me as anything but submissive. "Look, Suzanne, do you have access to Beverly's apartment?"

"Yes. The police have been there and gone. They dusted for fingerprints and took some of the photos of her old boyfriends and some of her sex toys, but two neighbors swore that Beverly was not at home Wednesday, and the police seem satisfied the condo is not the scene of the crime. They gave my aunt permission to deal with her stuff."

"Did they leave any photos of the old boyfriends?"

"Oh, sure. They only needed a couple of good shots of each guy, and Bev had tons. Talk about an ordeal for my aunt and uncle. I went over there with them. Bev never acted like Miss Innocent, but you know how blind parents can be. But even I was shocked by the photos. We all wondered where she got her money, but I didn't think she was into porn. Aunt Ruth practically fainted."

"Can we go to the condo tomorrow after work?"

"No problem. I have a key. How about four o'clock?"

# CHAPTER 8

"Bar food," David Shapiro whined at the suggestion of Seabright Brewery. "I can't eat that."

"This isn't for dining pleasure, this is for my investigation. I'll buy you a beer."

"Come to my house," he countered, "and I'll make you a killer margarita."

I had no desire to sip another person's margaritas since I considered my own par excellence. Furthermore, if I had a margarita at his place, there was a fair chance we'd never get out for dinner, unless the high-pitched keening of my stomach turned him off. Finally, there was the chance he wasn't just a horny guy, but a cold-blooded murderer.

Even with this possibility looming in my mind, I felt excited. Suzanne had made an accurate assessment of my emotional and physical states. I was ready for a transitional relationship. Or forget the relationship part, I was ready for sex. I was also now in that primal, hormonal part of my cycle that conspired against women and broke down resolve faster than margaritas.

"The margarita sounds delicious for another day," I said.

"Let's do this then. Let's go down to El Palomar and put our name on the list. Since it's Friday, there'll probably be an hour wait, and we can make a dash up to the Seabright Brewery while we're waiting."

"That's a plan. I'll meet you there."

When the light turned green, David's Escort shot forward.

I followed in my Ghia, but the suddenness of David's lane change left me breathless. I wondered if he (a) was showing off, (b) always drove like a maniac, or (c) was angry that I'd insisted upon separate vehicles. That was my one tiny safety precaution. It was not a myth that killers returned to the scene of the crime. David Shapiro's own "friend," Regina Smith, didn't trust him. I wondered about my sanity, palling around with the guy.

He'd dressed for our "date" in new black Levi's and a crisp white dress shirt. I was glad I'd upgraded my Levi's with a black velvet top. He'd accurately estimated the wait at El Palomar—forty-five to fifty minutes.

Now David drove over the San Lorenzo River. The levee rose above me until I crested a hill overlooking the mouth of the river emptying into the Pacific Ocean. Across the river the lights of the Boardwalk shimmered in the dusk. Screams from the riders on the roller coaster pierced the windows of my car.

When we reached the brewery, instead of turning toward its parking lot, David turned into a quiet, residential area. As I parked, I looked around the dark street. It was deserted.

My car door cracked. David Shapiro loomed above me.

"I hope you don't mind parking here," he said. "The parking lot is nuts."

I clutched my keys and kicked open the door.

David Shapiro jumped back. "What the fuck?"

I didn't bother explaining. As we walked, I kept six feet of distance between us, even though what he'd said was true. The parking lot had been ridiculously restriped—pinstriped—as though Americans drove Minis. Parking was a nightmare.

"I'll get my photos back from Long's tomorrow," he said.

"I'd like to see those."

"I thought you might."

When we reached some people waiting at the window of a burrito stand, relief washed over me, but I still kept distance between us.

"Would you mind walking with me?" David asked as we

crossed the intersection toward the brewery.

"Your pal Regina Smith didn't exactly sing your praises."

"Is that what's bugging you? Regina didn't want to model nude, but her mom pushed her into it and she blames me."

"Her mom?"

"Yeah. She runs a shitty facility and she thought if Regina modeled for me, I'd make sure my friend Leonard didn't cite them." He snorted at the idea. "Not that I knew that at the time."

The lighted patio of the brewery buzzed with people. Even over the traffic we could hear the collective murmur of conversations and the blues band wailing.

"Sounds like the Soul Drivers," I said, picking up my pace. I hadn't counted on this fringe benefit. A high quality local band, The Soul Drivers featured Terry Hancks on sax.

"So what's our mission?" David shouted over the music. Now that we were in the safety of a public place, I slowed up and let him close the gap between us.

I stopped, pulled on the sleeve of his black leather jacket and leaned close to his ear. His skin smelled like shaving cream. "I'm looking for a guy I saw Beverly talking to here. He's tall, over six feet, slender, dresses like a biker and has long grayish hair, braided last time I saw him."

"Isn't this about like betting on the Warriors?" David sounded cranky.

"The Seabright Brewery has a huge contingent of regulars."

"Okay," he said, as though granting permission.

The crowd on the patio was a mix of singles on the prowl, couples with their small children, and clusters of friends. I saw two guys I knew from volleyball and waved to them.

"You take the patio," David said. "I'll look inside."

"I want the inside."

"Why?"

"I love this band."

He shrugged, but obviously preferred to call the shots.

"Do you want your beer?" I asked.

"Naw. I'll take a pitcher of margaritas at El Palomar."

"The last time I saw this guy, he was near the wall of the building."

"Do you think he hasn't moved in the last couple of weeks?"

"People can be very territorial," I insisted.

Inside the bar, I staked out the short hallway that led to the bathrooms until I'd seen enough men come and go to be reasonably sure who occupied the men's room. In spite of the crowd, I could see the tall Terry Hancks, his thin body bowed and his shoulders hunched over his saxophone as the band blared *Shotgun*. Trays of food, lifted high, ported baskets of calamari, thick burgers with fries, salads topped with strips of grilled chicken. Saliva collected in my mouth.

Across the room David flagged me. Instead of trying to elbow my way through bodies, I pointed a finger to the exit near me to indicate I'd meet him on the patio.

I quickly saw why David had beckoned me. The man with the gray ponytail leaned on the stucco near where I'd last seen him with Beverly. In front of him, a burly friend sporting a red bandanna dangled a cigarette.

"Now what?" David asked as I met him near the fountain.

"I'm going to talk to the guy."

"What was that?" David wrinkled his forehead.

"Just my stomach."

"Want company?" David asked.

I shook my head.

"I'm going to be right here."

I smiled. The bearded guy with Beverly's friend looked like he could pick David up by the scruff of his neck and pitch him over the patio's wall. Still the protectiveness was sweet. Chad's protectiveness drove you crazy, I reminded myself as I neared the two men. David's protectiveness is different, I argued with myself. He didn't tell me not to go.

*He wants to protect you all right, until he can get you on that dark street and throttle the daylight out of you.*

"Hi," I said to Mr. Ponytail.

He inspected me up and down with infuriating indifference. His friend's eyes bore into the side of my head. His massive, tattooed arms looked powerful enough to rip off my head, and his disposition looked cheerful enough to do it. My knees felt loose. From hunger, I told myself.

"I'm Beverly's friend."

Mr. Ponytail's steely eyes flickered with recognition. "Oh, yeah. You was here with her cousin." He fingered his gray mustache, which was full and curled at the ends, but fell shy of a handlebar. "Sad," he shouted over the music and his eyes softened to charcoal. He planted one black boot back against the stucco, leaned his butt on his left hand and with his right, extracted a package of cigarettes from his vest pocket, pulled one out with his teeth, and lit it with one hand, flicking his thumbnail against the match.

I got close to him so that I wouldn't have to shout. "Could I ask you some questions about Beverly?"

"Police?"

The band had launched into a smoking version of *Walk the Dog*. I couldn't hear him, but read his lips.

I shook my head. Up close he was a good-looking guy, a planed face and lean muscles on his bare arms.

He bent close. "Private investigator?"

In the last six months without Chad, one thing I had not missed was smoker's breath. "Not yet. In training. Suzanne, the cousin, asked me to look into Beverly's death."

"T.J., buy me a Pale Ale," he commanded his henchman.

The big man glowered, but lumbered off.

He thrust a hand toward me. "Cole," he said.

"Carol Sabala." Cole had a strong, firm shake. I was definitely in a dangerous, hormonal state. Every man was shooting off electricity. "What were you talking about with Beverly the day I saw you together?"

"Shiiiit." He glanced toward the small line of people

outside the burrito stand across the street. Dusk was settling into darkness. "Ah, shit." He ground out his barely smoked cigarette on the concrete.

The music stopped. Inside, the sax player introduced the members of the band.

"I may as well talk to you," Cole muttered. "Good practice. The cops will be asking the same questions if they can locate me. 'Course by the time they pull their sorry heads from their asses, I'll be in Sturgis."

Having made this pronouncement, Cole didn't unburden his soul, but rather scanned the patio. "That your partner?" He nodded toward David, but I didn't turn around. "If he weren't such a shrimp, I'd think he was a cop."

"Nope. Just a suspect."

"Come with me over to my ride."

The low slung, black machine rested with six other motor-cycles between the patio and the café next door. We threaded our way into the darker and quieter spot. I was glad to have someone keeping an eye on us.

"Nice bike," I said.

He smiled, warm and slow, and patted the Harley.

"So what about you and Beverly?" I prompted. "Did you date?"

He smirked. "You might call it that."

"What did you call it?"

"Yeah, well, we called it dating, too. Beverly was a class act. She didn't let her customers feel cheap."

*Customers.* I remembered the day in the Employees Dining Room. *It could be good advertising.* Had Beverly been a hooker as well as a porn queen?

Cole laughed and lit another cigarette. "Shit. You didn't even know about Bev."

I was glad it was dark so Cole couldn't see the blush creeping up my neck. Everybody in this investigation seemed more sexually savvy than I was. I felt like an innocent in

Wonderland or the Land of Oz. I should go home and put my hair in pigtails.

"As you can probably tell, I'm not too shocked by her death. The police will have plenty of guys to choose from."

*Like you.*

Sometimes in life our needs are not very clear to us, but at this moment, mine crystallized. I needed food and I needed a less revealing face. "I knew she liked edgy sex."

He laughed, not cruelly, but at my expense. "Edgy. That's a new word for it." He took a thin wallet from the back pocket of his leather pants, extracted a business card and handed it to me.

I turned toward the patio for more light and read, "Cole Thomas. PussyTech." My stomach wailed.

"What was that?" Cole asked. "Sounded like a dying animal?"

"Just my stomach." I glanced up to see David, who made an elaborate pantomime of pointing at his watch and turning up both palms.

"Look, you should go eat, and I should go drink my beer. You can reach me at that e-mail address." He flashed a thin blade of smile. "Visit our website. You can find out a bit about Bev there."

# CHAPTER 9

David and I hustled by the statue of Tom Scribner who used to play a saw in the downtown mall. The El Palomar restaurant was located in what had once been a grand hotel. The rooms now served as low-income housing, but as with a fine lady, neither age nor circumstances could obliterate the hotel's air of stateliness and dignity. The restaurant occupied what had been the lobby. The receptionist had already called our name, but promised us the first table available.

We wended our way through the dimly lit restaurant to the noisy, well lit bar in the back, good for trolling and serious drinking. David pressed his way to the bar and ordered. It was past nine o'clock, long past my dinnertime. Past my bedtime. David hoisted the pitcher of margaritas over the shoulders of young men lining the counter and the bartender handed me the glasses, one salted, one not. The receptionist called our table.

We received a booth under a large, framed mural. The high, high ceiling made the restaurant seem fancy, but in reality it was a noisy, popular place with no tablecloths or view.

We gulped our margaritas and stuffed our mouths with warm tortilla chips. I chewed on my black swizzle stick because if I didn't slow up, I'd be plastered in two minutes flat.

The margaritas were good, but not as good as mine. My field of expertise was baking, but hanging around a kitchen all day had stuffed my head with plums of wisdom: you can't unsalt the soup; thyme is an underrated herb; and delicious margarita mix is an oxymoron.

David smacked his chips. "What I wonder is where Beverly put in her diaphragm."

I scooped up enough salsa to fill the curl in my chip. "She could have done it here," I said flippantly, dropping the delicious bomb into my mouth.

"This is the first place I thought of," David said seriously. "I mean think about downtown. Because of the homeless, a lot of stores have their restrooms locked. Customers only."

A slender, dark-haired waitress in a black mini skirt took our orders for *enchiladas de pollo a la parilla*. "Have you ever noticed how all the waitresses here are young and white?" David asked. "Only under-thirty babes need apply."

"Civil-rights suit waiting to happen," I quipped, not wanting to get into restaurant politics and all the possible explanations for the seeming discrimination. "Beverly could have been a customer anywhere," I said, "and there are plenty of unlocked restrooms—the bookstore, Espresso Royale, the Catalyst . . . ." I stopped because I couldn't think of any more.

"Of those, which settings are most likely to be the backdrop for sex and murder?"

"I see what you mean." Beverly probably didn't have a sexual tryst in Book Shop Santa Cruz. Plus alcohol often played a part in an organized murderer's act. "Are you suggesting I start canvassing all the bars in town?"

David refilled his drink. My head buzzed.

"Not all of them." His dark eyes sparkled with intelligence and alcohol-induced bravado. "The body wasn't moved. He killed her on the levee."

"How do you know that?"

"I'll show you in the photos tomorrow."

David's pushiness to see me again was both flattering and unsettling. What did he want? Was he interested in me or was he captivated by the murder?

"Exactly why did you take pictures of the crime scene?"

"Like Hillary said about Mount Everest: 'Because it was there.'"

"I can't look at them until late afternoon."

The waitress delivered our platters and we tore into our food. Shredded cabbage, guacamole, and sour cream heaped on top the enchiladas. For a solid five minutes, ravenous hunger beat out our inquisitive natures. Neither of us ate like we were on a first date. I motioned to David several times to wipe sour cream from his mustache. He came up for air first. "How about four o-clock at my place?"

His offer was too much like "Let me show you my etchings."

"I'll be down at the Yacht Harbor," I said. "How about if we meet at the Crow's Nest about five?"

"All right."

The food sopped up the tequila and my head stopped swimming. The police had collected boxes of evidence from Beverly's condo and then had opened it to the family. They seemed convinced that neither the meeting nor the murder had happened there. But how did David know Beverly hadn't met her date there?

"Why do you assume Beverly put in her diaphragm while out and about?"

"I'm sure with my personality this will come as a shock, but I have gone out with a number of women."

I smiled.

"If she'd inserted her diaphragm at home," he continued, "she would have left the case and gel there."

What surprised me was that Beverly used a diaphragm at all. It was a cumbersome form of birth control for a hooker and it didn't provide any protection against disease. Her choice suggested a select clientele—a call girl.

David shoveled rice and beans into a flour tortilla, and continued as if there'd been no interlude, "Since the body wasn't moved, Beverly and the killer must have been walking on the levee."

"That's not a very romantic place to walk."

"Exactly. So I'm thinking they probably didn't walk far. We should start our canvassing with the Catalyst."

"Are you thinking about canvassing *tonight?*"

"Sure."

He seemed full of energy. Obsessive. Obviously not someone who had to go to work at four a.m. "I don't even have a photo of Beverly."

"We could describe her. She was murdered on Wednesday night. The bars would not have been that busy."

I shook my head. "I can't do it tonight."

"You're right, though," he said. "We should start with the places closest to where I found her."

I didn't point out that this had been his idea.

"A woman would be on guard on the levee," he added.

"Not if she was drunk enough."

"True. Wouldn't it be nice if we had access to the autopsy results?"

I drained the last trickle of margarita in my glass. "What is this *we* business?"

He smiled. That wide, charming, nothing-to-hide, here-I-am smile. "Don't you think we'd make a great team? Nancy Drew and Frank Hardy?"

In the light of his smile, I had to hold on to the idea he could be the murderer, enticing another victim into his web. Even after Ted Bundy had been convicted, women had written him marriage proposals. I didn't want to be that sort of pathetic idiot.

# CHAPTER 10

"A man's home is his castle; a woman's home is her nest," I thought as I stared at my computer screen.

It was past eleven and in a few hours I'd be dressing for work. When David and I had left the restaurant, the late movies at the new Cinema 9 had been ending. People flooded the sidewalks and coffee houses. In its post-earthquake resurrection, downtown Santa Cruz felt cosmopolitan and vibrant.

Since he couldn't persuade me to canvass bars, asking folks if they'd seen Beverly on the night of her murder, he'd suggested that we walk the levee back to the scene of the crime.

"You've gotta be kidding."

He'd been dead serious.

The adrenaline rush still hadn't stopped even with Lola curled at my feet and all my doors locked. At least David didn't know where I lived.

On the computer I made a file for my case, labeled it *Beverly Homicide* and typed up notes on my investigation. Then I entered the PussyTech address. On the home page Beverly stood naked with her legs wide apart. Above her, red scrolled letters identified her as Randi.

A black leather band that looked specifically designed for simulated gagging covered her mouth. She wore black leather handcuffs. The same type, no doubt, my mom had seen in her neighbor's briefcase. Beverly, or Randi, held her linked wrists to the side so as not to block the view of her body. Black stiletto heels completed her attire. She looked beautiful, her hair and make-up completely undisturbed by whatever ravages she'd supposedly endured.

The text advertised horny blond women waiting for Sex! Sex! Sex! in every position, with links to bondage, S&M, watersports, spankings, Roman showers, and coprophilia.

I clicked on watersports. A small picture showed a woman, not Beverly, squatting over a naked man and urinating on his chest. The text held a standard warning: *This site contains explicit adult content. You must be over eighteen to view this free content. To continue, you must prove you are of legal age. Enter a valid credit card number so we can comply with the law. Then continue to enjoy for free. Your credit card will not be billed.*

I pressed the *continue* button without giving my credit card, but the computer looped back to the same screen.

What a joke. Kids could get the same eyeful I already had without a credit card, as if a credit card number would prove a thing anyway. A credit card number simply provided PussyTech with every bit of information they ever wanted, which wasn't your age.

I tried the link to Roman showers to educate myself. Roman showers featured a small photo of a naked woman vomiting on a prone, naked man. Half digested enchilada rose in my throat, sour. Any wild sexual fantasies I had didn't extend this far.

But how did one judge where healthy sexual fantasy stopped and sickness began? My mom found Klaus's handcuffs alarming; I found the idea of them somewhat erotic.

Again, I had to give my credit card number if I wanted to continue, so I clicked back to the home page, to Beverly standing, seductive and inviting. From what I'd learned so far about her, this venue might have provided pleasure as well as money.

Curiosity drove me to peek at coprophilia, which turned out to mean love of feces. I quickly backed out to the photo of Beverly. While I hadn't seen anything else featuring her, I had the idea of what she'd been up to. Nude modeling and possible prostitution had helped her to finance the Yacht Harbor condo and the shiny Miata. Maybe there *was* a way to buy out Chad, I thought wryly to myself.

Even though it was past midnight, I clicked to the University of California page to see what I could find out about Klaus Holthuis. At the faculty link, I typed in his name. This supplied his university address and e-mail, which I copied onto a clean sheet of paper with his name at the top. I went to the Language Department and learned that he was a visiting Professor of Linguistics and his areas of interest were semantics, logic, nihilism and German. Basic information.

The nihilism was interesting. Although I felt I knew what nihilism meant, I looked it up in Webster's anyway: *1 a: a viewpoint that traditional values and beliefs are unfounded and that existence is senseless and useless b: a doctrine that denies any objective ground of truth and esp. of moral truths.*

A good philosophy for a pervert. Or a murderer.

# CHAPTER 11

Four o'clock in the morning was a miserable time to go to work, especially after only three hours of sleep. I plodded up the steps to the loading dock and turned on the light in the hallway. As usual, I was the first employee to arrive. The place was so quiet I could hear the hum of electricity. As brutal as it was to drag myself to work at this hour, once I managed to wake up, I liked the solitude of the predawn.

To my immediate right was the Employees Dining Room. Since someone had once leapt from its doorway and clobbered me, I now passed on high alert with my shoulders up, although the chances of being attacked in the same way twice were about the same as lightning striking twice. I wondered if Eldon had found someone to replace Beverly and if any of the guys in the kitchen had known about Beverly's other job. I'd fish around at break.

I punched in. In the unisex locker room hung racks of uniforms. I searched for the hounds-tooth pants with the red Magic Marker slash on the inner pocket, my way of marking pairs that fit. I found a pair with a green dot. I smiled. Imitation is the sincerest flattery. Then I groaned.

Every time I thought in cliché, I worried that I was becoming my mother. I selected a white smock, donned my chef's cap, and hauled myself up the hallway. For no particular reason, I used my hip to bump through the swinging door into the kitchen.

"Stop!" a voice shouted.

I jumped. A barrel stuck in my back. The kitchen was ablaze with light.

"You almost hit me with that door."

I twisted my head. A tiny Asian man stood beside a mop bucket up to his thighs. The barrel in my back was the end of his mop handle. He'd used the handle like a martial arts stick to keep his face from being rearranged by the door.

"Sorry," I said. "You're running late."

"Two people called in sick."

At least I was now fully awake. Adrenaline was more effective than caffeine. I didn't stop at the bakery, but passed through the kitchen to the refrigerators. I unlocked the door of the first one and lugged a five-gallon bucket of Russian teacake dough to the bakery.

Russian teacakes, or Mexican wedding cakes, were one of the easiest items I made, but perennial favorites. To make perfect balls of dough, I borrowed the melon ball scoop from Suzanne's *garde manger* department.

The chink, chink, chink of the scoop on the tray created a soothing background for my thoughts. The rich scent of vanilla wafted from the dough, but it did nothing to dispel the rotten-tooth taste in my mouth. Was investigating really the right line of work for me? I wasn't squeamish about my foray into Pussytech. The scientist in me willingly contemplated how a model might protect her mouth from the bacteria of feces, if that was even happening. It might be all an illusion.

What appalled me weren't the images, but the idea that they appealed to some people.

Was I a prude, as Suzanne had teased?

Boundaries are natural, I reassured myself, even if I did ridicule the tight lines my mother drew around heterosexual sex. Without some censorship, one would be an anarchist . . . or a nihilist. A feral creature.

When Suzanne arrived, she came right to the bakery without changing into her uniform. She wore black sweats and the bright kitchen light washed out her face.

"You look like you had about as much sleep as I did," I commented.

"That good?" she said.

I checked the cookies in the oven and then took a huge stainless steel vat from a shelf. Today I was making a dark, slightly sweet bread known in the days before political correctness as squaw bread. Quickly, in a whisper, I filled Suzanne in on the meeting with Cole Thomas and what I'd learned of PussyTech.

"Well, that's no surprise," Suzanne said. "We knew she was doing something for extra money. And when we went through her condo, she had enough toys to open a small store." Suzanne glanced over her shoulder to make sure Eldon wasn't on the prowl. Now that she'd warded him off, she was no longer immune to being written up. "I never bought the idea Bev had a sugar daddy. She was too independent."

"That's the part I don't understand. She's an unlikely victim."

Suzanne leaned in close. She smelled strange. "Maybe she was playing a part. She could be the helpless little girl if that's what the guy wanted. You'll see what I mean at the condo this afternoon."

I sniffed Suzanne's honey-colored curls. "You smell like cologne." Perfume was forbidden in the kitchen. Suzanne wouldn't have dabbed it on herself; the scent had rubbed onto her.

She blushed.

"Hamad?" I guessed.

"I know it isn't right with Bev's death, but I couldn't help myself."

"In the face of death, wanting to be held is the most natural response in the world."

"Thanks."

In her vulnerable state, I could see Suzanne being sucked right into this relationship, and my kindness lasted less than a minute.

"So are you packing your bags to move to Kuwait? Or why bother. You'll need a whole new wardrobe to cover your flesh."

"Actually, Hamad *is* thinking about going back."

"I don't care if Hamad goes back. It's you that I don't want tiptoeing through the land mines."

"Nobody walks in their desert," she said in exasperation. "It's hotter than Nevada and twice as boring. They all ride in their gold Mercedes." She glanced into the kitchen. "I better get into uniform. I'll meet you at the condo about fourish. Here's the address." Since my hands were covered with flour, she slipped a folded yellow Post It into my smock pocket.

To my disappointment, Eldon was setting up the steam table in the Employees Dining Room. With the kitchen manager in the room, I would have to make sure I didn't exceed my allotted fifteen-minute break, although after what I'd learned about him on my last case, I suspected that Eldon was afraid to write me up. Consequently, I was more respectful of the fifteen-minute limit than I'd ever been in the past. I had no heart to exploit his anxiety.

The real danger here was allowing Eldon any inroad into the barrage of prattle that he mistook for conversation. I didn't even cross the room to get a cup of coffee, but rather sat at the table nearest the door.

I looked at the two guys taking a break—Todd and Ray. I knew them both, but not well. It seemed like I hardly knew anyone in the kitchen anymore, partly because of the Burn and Turn Policy—Burn 'em out and turn 'em over, and partly because the murder of our Head Chef Jean Alcee Fortier a few years ago had shaken up the entire staff.

Even though Todd was now a sous chef, I still thought of him as the-curly-haired-young-guy-who-gave-Fortier-mouth-to-mouth. And Ray was simply his-friend-the-front-line-cook. Maybe it was an age thing. The two guys were in their late twenties—young. Ray wore a goatee and sideburns. With my divorce, house worries, and onset of patellar tendonitis, I felt old.

I missed the delicious gossip about Jean Alcee Fortier and his latest sexual conquest. I missed a lot of people who'd previously worked in the kitchen, but more than that, I missed my place in a good ol' boy society. The old guard was gone; now I was the old guard and I didn't like it. Maybe it was time to move on.

I didn't have a clue what to say to these young guys, so I said, "What's up?"

Todd did the chin lift thing that qualified as a greeting among the young.

Ray said, "How's it going, Carol?"

I hated this, the way they threw the conversational ball back to me. This was the opposite extreme of talking to Eldon. They probably had about as much of an idea what to say to me as I had to say to them. Even though there was only eight or ten years between us, we'd grown up with different television shows, different music, and different fashions. I'm sure I looked very prudish and straight to them, like their moms. So, what the hell, I jumped in with both feet. "What do you guys think of Beverly's murder?"

"Are you going to investigate it?" Todd asked excitedly.

Was this the Generation X method of conversation? I ask a question, then they ask a question, spinning without answers into the new millennium. "Yes," I answered.

They both straightened in their chairs. Two sets of eyes flicked toward Eldon. Were they nervous that I might prolong their break and get them written up? Were they nervous about what I might ask? Or, were they simply nonplused because they couldn't think of a follow up question to *yes*?

I hated what I was about to do. If Beverly hadn't already sullied her reputation at work, I was about to do it for her. I rationalized that the information would soon be in the local paper, anyway.

I leaned in close and put my palms on the table. The two guys bent toward me, their eyes rolling warily to the right. I twisted to follow their gaze.

"Carol." A hammy hand landed solidly on my shoulder. I jumped back. "I just brewed some coffee, my special blend with cardamom. Smell it?" Eldon's smooth, bland face illustrated sniffing motions. "Want some?"

"I like my coffee unadulterated." I wanted Eldon literally off my back. This solicitation was apparently his new method of micro-managing me, but I preferred the old Eldon who hadn't been tentative, the one who would have been looking at his watch now and saying, "Carol, stop pestering these guys during their break."

"There's a big fat fly buzzing over the steam table," I said.

I think Eldon knew I was lying, but he hustled away. I felt both pity and irritation. He should know that I'd never blab around the secret I'd learned about him when I'd investigated a murder at Watsonville High School. On the other hand, if he decided to scale back my job to four days . . . .

"Where was I?" I asked the boys.

Ray smiled. He had crooked teeth, but looked adorable. *Hoo-boy*, I thought.

"Let's see," Ray said, "you had on your best tough-guy face and you were about to interrogate us."

Was I being teased? Flirted with? Were men like tomcats who could sniff a female in heat a mile away? Was I in danger of becoming part of the How-Stella-Got-Her-Groove-Back phenomenon of pushing-forty women with twenty-something guys? My face was burning.

Ray turned to Todd. "Where were you the night of the murder?"

"Before or after I was in bed with Beverly Levandowsky?"

"In your dreams," I snapped.

"Not as often as I'd like." But the light left Todd's eyes almost as soon as he said it. He scratched nervously at the side of his face. "That was shitty, joking around about Beverly. She was one of the friendliest people I ever met."

"How friendly?" I asked.

Todd's gaze fell to the floor. "We joked around. That was all." But his face flushed when he raised his head to plant his chef's hat back on his curly locks.

"And I'm engaged," Ray announced, rising from his chair. He was tall and broad-shouldered and smiled down at me with his crooked teeth. He *was* adorable. Encircled and protected by the magical purity of his young love, he thought he could flirt with older women and yet remain safe from our salivating lust.

# CHAPTER 12

After work, I made a pit stop at the house and reassured Lola that she was The World's Most Intelligent and Beautiful Cat in spite of the fact her belly was already distended. She'd always had a tendency to overeat, which was why I'd put her on a diet in the first place. "You are the Elizabeth Taylor of cats," I told her as I pulled on the freckled ear. The ear reminded me of the poem *Pied Beauty: Glory be to God for dappled things . . .For rose mole all in stipple upon trout that swim."*

I'd changed into my jeans, tee shirt and high-tops at work, but I was dying for a shower. My body felt dusted with flour like a loaf of franchessi bread. But the shower would have to wait. I was about to do something I'd always wanted to do and it had a strict time limit. Still I took a moment to listen to the one message on my answering machine.

There was nothing, just a light breathing. Since it was so hard anymore to get a live person at the other end of the line, crank messages seemed the logical evolution of crank calls. Then my mom said, "I never talked to one of these things before."

I wondered why she was talking to one now. My mom knew perfectly well when I worked. Why hadn't she called when I got home? Had she forgotten my schedule? That didn't seem possible; I'd been working the same hours for ten years. Panic seized me. My mother's normal eccentricities had an irritating charm, but my mother gone dotty would be more than I could handle.

"I got *his* social security number," my mom whispered. "Can you come down this afternoon to get it? That's all."

She hung up.

How positively annoying. Surely even if she'd never left a message before, she could figure out that it was polite to say goodbye. Furthermore, I didn't have time to see her that afternoon. As it was, when I met Suzanne at the condo, she'd be angry that I still hadn't contacted Mike, her number one suspect. I'd been too busy with my day job and investigating my suspects, David Shapiro and Cole Thomas.

And how the hell had my mom gotten this Holthuis guy's social security number? And what was I going to do about my mom's offer of ten thousand dollars? God only knew I wanted and needed the money, but how could I accept it? I couldn't imagine that my mom had a lot to spare. She'd probably made a sizable chunk from selling the house, but she looked like she could live another twenty years. She'd need the money. There wasn't much chance that I'd become rich and be able to support her. Especially if she was growing senile.

All these pesky questions made me lose track of what I was doing. I stood in front of the bathroom sink and stared in the mirror to center myself. The reflection was frightening.

Genetically, I'd received good material, but under my blue-green eyes I now had two permanent bag lines. I'd had the crease in my forehead for some time, but new wrinkles were insinuating themselves at the sides of my full lips. If I twisted my head the right way, my neck puckered into chicken skin. Aging sucked. It meant that age-appropriate guys didn't have cute goatees but rather eyebrows that grew in uncontrollable ways.

Not that I didn't deserve every fold and furrow. I did nothing to protect my skin from the sun and I worried incessantly.

I took a moment to brush my teeth and to wipe off my face with a warm washcloth. I applied some mascara and a touch of lipstick. My face looked brighter. Still old, but brighter.

I raced to Long's with my '66 Karmann Ghia rattling. To

blot out my thoughts, I listened to *Orinoco Flow* cranked to full volume and opened my windows to take in the warming, fresh air off the Pacific. I did indeed like that baking allowed me to be off work by noon. On the other hand, as I turned into Long's parking lot and bee-lined to the film department, the investigation I was doing now didn't even seem like working, while baking had a tote-that-barge, lift-that-bale feel.

I approached the moment I'd often fantasized. I turned the corner to the drawers full of photos waiting for their owners. I went to S for Shapiro and flipped to the last number of his street address. There was nothing there.

I looked up nervously and riffled through all the S's. Still nothing.

I flagged a green apron. The sale's clerk had long blond hair and looked all of fifteen.

"Have today's pictures been delivered?" I looked into the reflective dome mirror to see if anyone hidden in a corridor were watching me.

The clerk gave me a smile full of blue braces and pointed at a basket across from the drawers, stuffed with photo envelopes. "We haven't had time to organize them yet," she said. "We don't really consider them ready for pickup until two, but you're welcome to look for yours if you'd like to."

I dug frantically, but before I could find David Shapiro's envelope, I came to another that stopped me cold: Chad Brown. My former husband. This made no sense. Chad didn't take pictures. Brown may have been a name common as dirt, too common for me to have ever adopted, but I felt sure there was only one *Chad* Brown in Santa Cruz.

The penmanship looped the letters and claimed him. This was his name written by the hand of his new girlfriend. My stomach knotted.

Our divorce had sailed cheaply through a legal service, no lawyers, and little acrimony. But after the fact, I'd learned that Chad had a crush on the twenty-five-year-old receptionist at the roofing company where he worked. Chad had not acted on his crush until we were separated, but clutching the photo pouch, I felt deceived all over again. He'd allowed me to believe that the divorce was solely my idea and I resented assuming all the guilt.

I glanced up into the mirror. No one seemed to be nearing the photo section except a chubby woman with a toddler, certainly not Chad's new girlfriend.

The gluey tab easily lifted. I slid the inner envelope from the package and looked up nervously. In the first photo they stood holding hands on West Cliff Drive, the Boardwalk far in the background. Chad had a smug smile playing on his lips. "Like a cat that's been in the butter," my mom would say.

The New Girlfriend was petite, much smaller than I was, maybe five foot two, with smooth skin and dark, straight hair to her butt.

"Excuse me."

I nearly jumped out of my skin.

The chubby woman clutching the hand of her small daughter gave me a dubious look. "Could we get by you to go through the photographs?"

"Sure," I said absently. I moved to the counter. This was torture, no less harrowing than being buried up to my neck, my head covered with honey, and the ants coming to take their first exploratory nibbles. But I couldn't stop.

I slipped the photo to the back and looked at the next. It was worse. The Girlfriend alone. She was sitting on the steps, presumably of wherever they lived. She wore cutoffs, a white tee shirt and athletic shoes with prissily rolled down white socks. Her elbows were propped on her golden thighs and her hands cupped a delicate chin. Her smile was broad and happy and full of white teeth and her dark hair sprayed down around her forearms.

As though I were trapped, I went to the next photo. It was worse. Chad stood straight and awkward and completely naked in front of a brass bed covered by a puffy, flowered comforter and many velvety pillows. The ants nipped at the corners of my eyes.

God. I remembered what Chad felt like. The muscles of his back. The strong arm draped over my naked waist. The residual smell of roofing tar clinging to his hair. My lips twitched and contorted in pain.

The ants marched into my ears, driving me mad and I went to the next photo. Her again. Sitting sedately on the edge of the bed dressed in only black thigh highs, tiny black undies and a see-through black bra. Clearly I wasn't the only one in our relationship who'd had unfulfilled fantasies. Why had Chad ever stayed with me when he could have her?

I choked and remembered that Chad hadn't left me; I'd pushed him away.

"Well this is a small world."

My head jerked up. For a moment, I felt uncertain of where I was. The items around me—cameras, boxes of film, the plastic wrap on photo albums—all glistened as though there'd been rain. I hastily closed the container of photographs and slid them back into the envelope.

A shimmery mirage of David Shapiro materialized in front of me. I should have been a little frightened. He could have caught me going through his photographs. But I felt only a little sick, as though the ants had marched down my esophagus and were starting to eat me from the inside out.

I had no idea how long I'd been standing there. The woman and child were gone and the teenaged clerk with the blue braces was sorting through the packages of photographs.

"Are you okay?" David asked.

I nodded. I was glad I'd put on the touch of make-up, although the mascara was probably smeared.

"You look as though you've been crying."

"I'm okay."

"Do you want to pay for those and go out for some coffee or something?"

"Ah . . . no. Let's just meet at the time we had planned. I have to do a little more shopping." I turned abruptly with my illicit package of photos and walked down the aisle of liquor, away from David Shapiro. I looked into the mirror only to see him examining me in it.

*Shit,* I thought. I gave him a little wave and watched until he turned to the drawer with the S's. His envelope had already been filed.

I meandered along the back of the store—cleaning products, the pharmacy, over to the personal grooming, as far from the photo department as I could get. What if Chad or his new girlfriend popped over to Long's on a Saturday afternoon to pick up their photos? I started to sweat.

I inspected the dental floss—plain, waxed, tape, cinnamon-flavored, mint-flavored, Long's brand. My mom had been a dental hygienist, so I wondered if there was something Freudian about the place I'd decided to stop.

What wealth and selection. The smile of Chad's new girlfriend appeared like the Cheshire Cat's. I wanted to torture myself with another peek at her photo, but instead I pressed the envelope to my stomach, concealing the name.

I stood there in my reverie, resisting paranoid thoughts of Chad and his new girlfriend chasing me through Long's. How did we become such a spoiled country that we supported twenty different varieties of dental floss? I felt awash in plastic packaging and hard, unbiodegradable containers and slightly nauseous in the sea of overwhelming consumerism. Usually, I experienced these attacks only in the big box stores like Home Depot or Wal-Mart. All the stuff. All the sacrificed trees, planned obsolescence and ultimate landfills. The values behind the rows and rows of choices somehow seemed connected to Beverly's murder.

"I like Glide, myself."

Holy cow, what was wrong with me? Had I forgotten that this guy was persistent? Had I forgotten that, like me, he was an investigator? Had I let it slip my mind, that all that aside, he was a guy who for some reason wanted to go out with me? Maybe to choke the life out of me. Remember his bizarre suggestion of a little stroll along the levee? Had I really thought that he'd simply pay for his photos and leave?

"Actually, Long's version of Glide," he said. "Why pay more, right?" He slid a package off its hook for me.

I froze like a bunny sensing its predator.

"No, no," I finally protested. "I don't want that."

He frowned. He'd probably been watching me stand in what appeared to be paralyzed indecision for the last minute.

"I . . . . I . . . . this is embarrassing, but I forgot my money." I wheeled. "I have to put these pictures back."

"I could loan you some money," David Shapiro offered. "You could pay me back when we see each other later."

"That's okay," I said and marched away.

He galloped beside me, smile blazing. "Surely it's not my relentlessness or enormous capacity for negativity that's making you act this way."

*Ah, as my mom would say, this is a fine kettle of fish.*

If I hadn't needed to hide from David Shapiro my original reason for being in Long's Photo Department, which was to snoop through his photos, I would have told him the truth. He seemed like the type of guy, perhaps the only person I knew, who could appreciate what I'd done.

Instead, I chased him away with a stick. "Have you ever thought about placing one of those personal ads?"

He stopped and assessed me. "Are you asking because of the case or because you want me to get lost?"

He found his own answer. "Just for your information, I already have an ad." He turned and walked to the door.

# CHAPTER 13

Once again ensconced in the prickly splitting seat of my car, I felt better. If I hurried, I could work in the visit to my mom before I met Suzanne at Beverly's condo.

I maneuvered up 41st Avenue, which was glutted with traffic. A black Explorer turned onto the freeway ahead of me, blocking any view of the road. The vehicle cost a fortune, guzzled fuel, and had a bumper useless for anything but sporting its gold I'd-rather-be-shopping-at-Nordstrom's license-plate holders. I was willing to bet the money for my house that the four-wheel-drive monster had never seen a day off pavement.

Risking my life, I pulled around the SUV. Except for an occasional yearning for an air bag, I was content with my rattletrap. The low insurance, great mileage, and home repairs on the simple engine were part of the reason I had the possibility of owning a home as a single person in Santa Cruz.

Now that I could see the highway, my mind drifted toward more pleasant thoughts of the handsome Klaus Holthuis. For all my mom's fretting, he was a university professor, which meant he'd been fingerprinted and given at least a cursory background check before he was hired.

In ten minutes, I was turning the key chime in the door of the Hinds House.

Hearty and blond, Klaus Holthuis filled the doorway. Since I'd only moments ago been visualizing us together doing a little hanky-panky, my cheeks flamed with heat.

"Good afternoon," he said.

A person interested in nihilism should look more like

a skinhead. He should have leathery skin or a jagged scar from eye to chin. Instead, in spite of the warm weather, he was wearing slacks and a dress shirt, sleeves rolled down and buttoned.

Klaus made a little bow and waved me in. "Has my coffee tempted you back?" The aroma filled the foyer.

A person interested in nihilism also should seem less concerned with the finer things in life.

"Would you and your mother care to join me?" he asked.

I cared to, all right. "I can't. I have another appointment in a while and I have to discuss some business with my mom." *Regarding you.*

"Perchance we'll have another opportunity."

"Perchance."

I watched the strong back retreat to the kitchen. *What the hell is wrong with me?* He had extended an opening to suggest another time, and I'd dismissed him. David Shapiro had pursued me through Long's and I'd insulted him.

I took the steps two at a time, punishing myself. If I were still playing volleyball regularly, I wouldn't be panting; on the other hand, if I were still playing volleyball regularly, every step would have sent a stab of pain up my knees.

Outside my mom's door, a two-foot statue of Saint Francis now stood sentinel. My mom was not religious, but the little birds on his arm would have appealed to her. The statue was not new, and this being Santa Cruz, someone had painted St. Francis's face blue, his robes red and the birds bright yellow, so the whole thing looked like it belonged in a Jamaican taxi.

My mom opened the door before I knocked. She appeared quite fetching in a hat made from a plastic bottle covered with red crochet. I couldn't wait for the liberating age when I felt free to wear anything. Then it occurred to me that according to Generation X, I probably already had. My mom glanced at her statue and beamed at me. "Do you like him?"

"Holy Saint Francis!" I exclaimed.

"I found him at the greatest thrift store over on Front Street."

"Are you planning to go out?" I asked since she was wearing a hat and had apparently slathered herself with sunscreen that smelled like coconut. I could imagine the girls on the street coveting my mom's retro-looking polka-dotted pullover.

"I thought after we confer that I'd sit in one of the lovely little yards here."

Someone should warn the ownership. If there was soil, my mom would want to garden, but she was as likely to plant potatoes as roses. Many of her habits had been formed by growing up during The Depression and then scrimping for years as a single parent.

"So how were you able to get Klaus's social security number?" I whispered, plopping into her wicker chair.

My mom sat on her bed. "Why are you whispering?"

"Klaus is downstairs."

"Oh, dear." She swallowed and I could see where I'd inherited the tendency toward a chicken-skin neck.

"Oh dear?" I asked.

My mom extracted an envelope from the drawer of her bedside table and handed it to me. The name Klaus Holthuis and his Hinds House address showed through the window. The return address was for a health care provider.

"He has the same coverage I used to have. Their statements list the patient's social security number."

"I'm not going to open it. Tampering with the federal mail is a felony!" I tossed the letter toward her as though it were a hot-cross bun.

My mom pulled her basset-hound look. All her polka dots drooped toward the floor.

She dug around in her pocket and in disgusted silence handed me a folded scrap of paper.

I unfolded the paper and there was the nine-digit number.

"You already opened it?"

She nodded gravely.

I got out of the chair and picked up the envelope. I inspected it. Completely intact. "Wow."

The polka dots rose like champagne bubbles. "Remember Bart?"

There'd been only one Bart in my life, my high school sweetheart. He'd been too old for me, already floundering around in the real world. He had brown hair down to his scrawny pectoral muscles, rode a motorcycle, had a tattoo of a lion on his shoulder, and smoked dope, everything outwardly to strike peril in the heart of a mother. Contrary to his image, he'd been a tender lover who'd helped me get on birth control pills. He'd also been literate and wrote me copious letters. Way too romantic for me.

"I had some practice," my mom said.

I blushed to think of all the nonsense my mom had read. She'd never said a word, had never let on. "Wow," I said again. "Amazing." I certainly didn't have my mom's duplicity. Maybe one perfected it through being a parent. Parent was a demanding role. One lived in constant proximity to one's kids for years and years and yet remained a complete mystery to them.

I told my mom what I'd learned so far about Klaus.

"Not much," she said. "But it's a start. I found out that before he came here last semester, he taught at Humboldt State."

Humboldt State was less than an hour from Ferndale. "He's practically kin, mom."

"Ten thousand dollars, Carol," she said without a smile. "The offer still stands."

# CHAPTER 14

Downstairs I saw how my mom had gotten Klaus's medical notice. Off to the side of the main entrance, open slots held each resident's mail. Like the self-serve photo drawers at Long's, the system belonged to a bygone era of innocence.

Klaus came out of the kitchen for my departure. "I hope we shall meet again."

From an American, "shall" would sound snooty, but from a foreigner, it sounded enchanting.

"I'm sure we shall."

Another gambit brushed aside. Snooping through Klaus's mail and envisioning him in fantasies made it hard to proceed like normal. Drat my mother, anyway.

"I'll keep my eye . . . ." He stopped. "Is it eye or eyes?" He ran a hand through his wavy golden hair.

"Either way."

"I'll keep my eye on your mother."

Not too carefully, I hoped.

I sped up the street to catch Highway 1. I had to make a phone call before I could face Suzanne. Fortunately my house was more or less on the way to Beverly's condo.

At the sound of the Karmann Ghia turning the corner, Lola hopped over the redwood fence. When I climbed from the car, she brushed up against my leg. No howling piteously now that she could overeat to her heart's content.

There was a phone message from the real estate agent who wanted to talk me into listing the house. I punched in the number Suzanne had given me and received the answering machine of Mike Taylor.

I couldn't imagine a murderer named Mike Taylor. It was a name for the boy next door, the captain of the football team, or the clerk at the auto parts store. On the other hand, the name fit perfectly with *the neighbors'* profile of a murderer: *He seemed like a regular guy. He kept to himself, but he was always polite.*

I left Mike Taylor a message explaining that I was a friend of Suzanne Anderson, investigating the murder of Beverly Levandowsky. He'd no doubt already been interviewed by the police and my call would be no great surprise.

I returned to my faithful Ghia and zipped toward the Yacht Harbor. Suzanne's yellow bug was parked on the street outside of Beverly's condo complex. I squeezed right between it and the red curb for the fire hydrant, going where no SUV had ever gone before.

Beverly's condo was near the street, less view of the upper harbor and fewer bucks. I rapped on the door that had been left ajar, called hello, and entered. Surrounded by piles of photo envelopes, Suzanne sat cross-legged on the oatmeal-colored Berber carpet.

It was probably my own superstitious projection, but sometimes scenes related to crimes vibrated with palpable evil. Beverly's condo was the opposite. Sunlight poured in from the street-side windows, and out the sliding glass door to the balcony one glimpsed the rocking boats in the harbor. The center piece of the living room was a large, cream colored leather couch and the interior design ran toward yellow and light blue—cheerful calm.

Suzanne waved me down next to her. She was stacking floppy disks.

"What are these?" I picked up one labeled "Cheesecake."

"More photos." Suzanne was dressed in the same black sweats she'd worn before work, her hair bunched in a rat's nest atop her head. "I think they were like Beverly's resumes."

"If she sent these out, what would keep some schmuck from posting them on a website, maybe setting up a money-making peep show?"

"I don't know. Maybe she did have that problem. Or maybe they weren't her resumes."

"Maybe she tried to do something about exactly that problem and the guy killed her."

"Maybe." The lack of protest, the lack of insistence that Mike had been the murderer, were not good signs. They indicated a turn from anger to depression. This may have been a natural progression that moved toward acceptance of Beverly's death, but anger was more conducive to my investigation.

Like the floppies, the packets of photographs were labeled. The first said *Girl-Girl*.

I slid out the photos. If I hadn't already been on the floor, you could have knocked me over with a feather. A boudoir—given to wine-red fabrics, black lace and dangling glass beads formed the background.

"That's Beverly's bedroom," Suzanne explained, pointing up the stairs.

"Oh, no, that's not why I'm sitting here in dumbfounded amazement."

Nor was it the sight of Beverly on all fours wearing black thong underwear.

"It's this other woman. I know her."

"You do?"

"I met her at David Shapiro's house. She was modeling nude for him. Her name is Annie."

Suzanne heaved a sigh. "That doesn't seem very amazing to me. I imagine it's a small group of people into this stuff. They probably all know each other."

I shuffled through the photos. Compared to what I'd seen on-line, they were pretty tame. Annie and Beverly lying entwined on the velvety bedspread and kissing.

I glanced at Suzanne. If I were to choose a female partner,

she'd be the one. I liked her. She was wonderful to hug and her skin felt like rose petals. But the idea of sex with a woman just didn't excite me.

"Have you ever thought about being with a woman?" Suzanne asked, as though she'd been tripping around in my thoughts.

I blushed. "Not really."

"I've heard that we're all bi-sexual, but most of us are trained not to respond to the same sex."

"Have you ever had a relationship with a woman?"

"Not a relationship, but remember Patsy?"

That was like asking if I remembered the 1989 earthquake. Patsy was a tattooed, buffed, Harley-riding, self-described *dyke* who'd worked for years as a pastry chef at Archibald's.

"She made a pass at me."

"What happened?"

"We were both in the locker room changing into our uniforms. Patsy asked me if I were curious what it was like being with a woman. I said, 'Yeah.' She backed me against the wall, put her arms on both sides of me and kissed me."

"On the lips?"

Suzanne rolled her eyes. "Where else?"

"Then what?"

"She asked if my curiosity was sated."

"And . . . ?"

"And it was."

"What did it feel like?"

"It was scary exciting, but not erotic exciting."

Beverly's sexual boldness got her killed, I thought. Still, Chad had forecast death or something worse for my adventurous spirit, and I'd never let that stop my investigating. Fear cut the heart out of living.

"Beverly was always like this." Suzanne cast her hand over the stack of photo envelopes. "When she was in high school, she'd buy lacy black panties and then show them off to me—not just hold them up. She'd put them on and strut around."

Suzanne plucked up an envelope labeled *Girl*. "Remember when I told you that Beverly might have seemed submissive to the killer?" Suzanne slid out the photos.

The first snapshot showed Beverly naked except for a tight, sleeveless white eyelet blouse that did its best to flatten her ample breasts. Her hair was tied up in pigtails. One arm wrapped around a huge white teddy bear and with her free hand she held a half-eaten banana.

I flipped through the pile.

"The problem with this shit . . ." Suzanne unfolded her body, stood and stretched.

My head jerked up because Suzanne seldom swore.

". . . is that when the police cruise the Internet and catch pedophiles, these sickos can use the defense, 'I thought she was an eighteen-year-old posing as a twelve-year-old. I swear to God, judge, I didn't know she was a minor.'" Suzanne padded to the kitchen area and slammed a kettle on the stove.

"I don't think Beverly's audience was pedophiles."

"Of course not. Beverly's our age. But imagine certain eighteen-year-olds in those shots."

"I see your point." If an eighteen-year-old could be made to look as though she were ten, then a pedophile could argue that he thought his ten-year-old was really eighteen.

"Want some tea?"

"Sure."

"Tension Tamer sound okay?"

"Perfect."

The package labeled *Fellatio*, to my relief, didn't show any guys I recognized.

I was getting tired. Even though Beverly looked primped and perfect in every shot, she'd been far sexier in real life. Maybe photographs did steal the soul. Something was lost in the static images. "This stuff is completely engrossing," I sighed, "for about ten minutes."

"Tell me about it. I've been going through Bev's things for the last couple of days trying to figure out what to do with it. Her parents don't want it and it's not exactly appropriate for the Salvation Army." Suzanne plunked a couple of mugs onto the counter. "Could you use a vibrating penis or a cock ring?"

"Nah, I think I'm set." A month ago my comment would have garnered anything from encouragement to get back on the playing field to a sarcastic suggestion that I could use the cock ring for my solitary napkin holder. But in the days since Beverly's death, Suzanne had abandoned any allusions to dating. Her face muscles sagged from not smiling.

"Bev's closet upstairs is better stocked than the Camouflage downtown. Her poor parents. I doubt they've ever been in Camouflage, so they have no idea how mainstream all this is. And like you said, kinda boring."

*Her poor parents* was right. They not only had to absorb a new image of their daughter, but also had to suffer without closure as the body remained at the morgue, the investigation continued, and the murderer roamed at large. *Selecting his next victim.* Because the murder had the markings of a type that would be repeated.

Suzanne carried two steaming mugs to the glass coffee table.

The next batch of photos was labeled *Tough Stuff* and featured Beverly in various absurd leather get-ups. She used the same costumes for *Bondage*, but added gags and ties. "Your cousin was quite versatile."

"You've only seen a fraction of her body of work," Suzanne said sardonically, the closest she'd come to a joke in days.

"What about the boyfriends?" I tested the tea. With the first hot mouthful, my tension slipped a notch. "I'd like names and pictures of all the guys the cops were interested in."

"The two in *Fellatio* are easy. The dark one, Jim, was a policeman from San Jose. He died about six months ago."

"Did he get shot?"

"Don't get excited. There's absolutely no connection between his death and Beverly's. He was a guy Bev liked. I actually met him. Nice guy. He died in a scuba diving accident in Monterey Bay."

I drank some more of the tea and rolled my shoulders.

"He got caught in a strong undertow and couldn't get into shore."

My brother Donald suddenly paraded in front of me. Dark like this guy Jim. Dead like this guy Jim. And my mind overloaded by the photos, naked like this guy Jim.

Heat crept up my neck. Our mother was not the type to allow her children to run around without diapers, and as teens Donald and I had been sullenly guarded about our bodies, so I couldn't remember ever seeing Donald fully naked until my mom and I were going through his effects after his death.

Then there had been the photos. Not like these, but snapshots here and there of Donald and his lover with their arms around each other at some hot springs. My brother's buns on a beach, his head propped up and grinning, his perfect chest hair turned toward the camera.

Suzanne scooted next to me and put her arm around me. "What's the matter?"

"What?" The molecules of my body regrouped and I found myself sitting on a carpeted floor holding a warm mug of tea.

"You're crying."

"I am?"

I wiped at the corner of my eye and sure enough, there was a tear. "It's the Tension Tamer."

Suzanne squeezed me. "It's okay. We all have plenty to cry about."

What a good friend I had. Another tear, one of gratefulness, trickled down my cheek.

# CHAPTER 15

The Crow's Nest sat at the mouth of the Santa Cruz Yacht Harbor. The restaurant/bar had been built during a time when good taste prevailed. A two-story building of dark brown wood, it nestled into its surroundings rather than thrusting pretentiously and cutting off everyone else's ocean view.

At this hour, the upstairs bar was only moderately busy and David waited for me at a window table. He had finished about half of his pale beer.

"Been waiting long?"

"Ten minutes." He twirled the packet of photos. He clearly did not like to wait, in spite of the view of sailboats breezing between the stone jetties to exit the harbor. Out beyond that, the ocean, Santa Cruz Municipal Wharf and the fancy houses of West Cliff Drive, curving along the cliffs of the bay.

I surveyed the drinks menu and ordered an expensive, exotic house specialty called Sunset at the Beach. *Just because.*

David took out his photos. He seemed content to ignore our run-in at Long's, which was fine with me, but I sighed involuntarily at the prospect of inspecting more photographs.

"Long day?"

For a second, I glared suspiciously, thinking he might be making a stupid pun reference to Long's, but then realized I was in hyper-vigilant, borderline paranoid, investigator mode. "Yeah, really long."

The young blond waitress wore a short black dress, and while she delivered my drink, David scanned the accentuated flat stomach and perky breasts. While he was only doing what I felt most men would do, he was irritatingly obvious.

I sipped my Sunset at the Beach, which tasted entirely too much like punch. Without restraint, I could suck the glass dry in about one minute, a problem since I couldn't recall having any lunch. That happened to me when I got involved.

"Tomorrow I might turn these over to the police," David said, nudging the photos to me, "but I thought I'd show them to you first."

"Aren't the police going to think you're a shady character? Obstructing justice and all that."

David shrugged. "They'll be irritated, but remember I'm an investigator. I've been working for the State Department of Social Services, investigating community care facilities, for twenty-two years. I'm called in when someone charges that something serious, like physical abuse, is going on at a facility. If I can substantiate the allegation, then the police get involved. So the guys downtown know me. They don't regard me as one of the boys in blue, more like an ugly stepbrother. But I'm still part of the family. Besides that, I'm not even sure I'll do it. They have their own shots."

I took another pull on the straw and found the fortitude to look at the first image. It was simply a shot of the levee, showing the backs of the stores along Front Street.

"These are distance shots for orientation," David explained. "That's the way you shoot a crime scene."

I slid the photo to the bottom of the stack. The next photo showed the levee and the wild anise growing along its edge, and the next traveled through the plants to the body.

Then came a mid-range series like the photograph in the local newspaper, but from various angles: Bev splayed on the ground, her dress hitched to the top of her legs, the contents of her purse spewed into the weeds beside her golden hair. David's photos revealed colors and details. I could make out every item: tissues, open wallet, tampons, diaphragm container, pill bottles . . . .

"Notice her clothing," David said. "I think the lifted skirt was arranged, but everything else looks consistent with struggling and falling down right there. When bodies are moved, it often seems to me that the clothes don't look natural. They're either too askew or overly straightened. That's more intuitive than scientific."

Even though I'd looked at the newspaper photo many times, with David's photos I noticed the tattoo on Beverly's ankle above skimpy sandals. Her skirt was black and the blouse a lacy maroon that you would have been able to see through if it hadn't come with a built-in black camisole. "In this outfit, I don't think she was planning to walk along the levee."

"Agreed."

When I came to the close-up shots, David walked around the table and sat beside me. He draped an arm along the back of my chair, leaned close with his faint scent of shaving cream, and pointed at the surreal white arm. "If I'd moved the body, you'd be able to see the lividity clearly, but even like this," his fingernail traced the bottom of the arm, "you can see it and it's completely consistent with the way she's laying."

"Weren't you tromping all over the crime scene when you were taking these?" *What better way for the murderer to explain away his hair and fibers?*

"Speaking of tromping." He tried to move the photo of Beverly to the bottom of the stack. My fingers clamped.

It annoyed him that I had control of the pace. I knew his type. Regardless of how many people were watching a television, he would end up with the remote guarded in his hand. Still my heartbeat quickened when his arm grazed my back.

He reached across the table to retrieve his beer. "Would you please go back to my orientation shots," he said with strained patience.

I spread the bottom photos along the table.

"Now, see, speaking of tromping, notice how there's no broken trail through the brush. If someone had dragged a body in or even tried to walk carrying a dead body, I'd expect to see more of a trail."

He waited, his mouth turning down at my lack of gushing appreciation for his deductive brilliance.

"Look, Carol, I discovered the body. The police *expect* my presence to have contaminated the scene. But I'm still going to come clean to my buddies downtown."

"That's virtuous."

His sharp dark eyes inspected me for irony.

"The problem here is not you, David. It's me."

"Oh great, Carol. That's a line guys like to hear."

Maybe it was the long day. The pictures of Chad. The memories of Donald. My awkwardness with David and then Klaus and then with David, again. Blame it on Tension Tamer chased with Sunset on the Beach and not enough sleep. I felt like shredding his photos and tossing them like confetti, but settled for telling him to fuck off.

David placed a protective hand on the stack of photos. "I usually have to pay women to talk to me like that," he said.

I smiled in spite of myself. I slipped the photo of Beverly to the bottom of the stack and looked at a close-up of objects from the purse.

"Look at this," he said excitedly, pointing.

"A swizzle stick?"

"Exactly. So, you see, I was right. They were at a bar before heading off for their walk."

"Looks pretty generic." The black straw swizzle was exactly like the one I was using to guzzle my Sunset at the Beach. "It could be old."

"Thanks," he said. "I thought I had a lead. Thanks for letting me know I'm just a moron posing as an investigator."

"No. That's me. You seem to know exactly what you're doing."

"Then why not team up with me?"

*Because you're a suspect.*

"You can't have Nancy Drew and Frank Hardy before you have Nancy Drew. Know what I mean?" I stared out the window at a flock of hundreds of shearwaters over the water following what must have been a school of anchovies.

The cocktail waitress swooped by our table and gave me a friendly smile. "Care for another?"

I shook my head and David passed, too.

"Is there any chance I could get Annie's address or phone number from you?"

"Annie? Why do you want to contact Annie? What information are you holding out on me, Carol?"

"It's one of those betting-on-the-Warriors moves," I said.

"Did she know Beverly?" he aggressively waved over the cocktail waitress. He could have been snapping his fingers.

"Change your mind?" she asked sweetly.

"Not recently," David said, picking up the pen from her tray. He scribbled a number on a napkin and handed it to me. "I'd give you an address, too, but I don't know where she lives."

"Do you know her full name?"

"Annabel Heather Smith."

The young waitress hovered and he waved her away.

I looked around for a clock. Normal people were off work for the weekend, or getting off work. They were taking showers, watching the news, thinking about dinner. As any good telemarketer would tell you, it was time to make calls.

David extended his wrist. "Check it out. Waterproof. In case I forget to take it off when I snorkel. Time here—6:06." He pressed a button. "Time in Venezuela—10:06."

"Why Venezuela's time?"

"Good question. If I'd known better, I wouldn't have gone there. It's a pit of a country, especially Caracas."

He again draped an arm casually around the back of my chair. The skin under my shirt buzzed with electricity.

"About one third of the country's twenty-two million people live in Caracas," he said. "They abandoned their farms and moved to the city during the oil boom. Then the boom went bust, and you got present day Caracas where it's best to take off your jewelry before walking around."

A huge part of me wanted to order another Sunset at the Beach, get slightly sloshed, and listen to this man tell tales about Venezuela.

# CHAPTER 16

At home Lola was as adorable, the walls as bare, and the refrigerator as empty as they had been the day before. I took out the jar of black olives and probed, but my fingers swam through liquid. I dumped the contents down the drain.

No wonder Chad had found a younger woman with black lingerie; she probably charbroiled cheeseburgers for him. Au gratin potatoes from scratch. Fresh green salad and corn on the cob. Homemade cheesecake.

When I'd first been with Chad, I used to make him meals like that. But I was like the mechanic with an old beater or the carpenter with the run-down house. After a few years at my job, the last thing I'd felt like doing at home was working in the kitchen.

I poked around in the cupboard to see if there was anything edible in a can. I found some tuna, but had no bread or crackers that could be considered remotely fresh.

Since I could eat breakfast and lunch at work for free, I had less incentive than a normal person to stock my larder.

I gave up for the moment and went to check my messages. I had one from Mike Taylor. He sounded tired, but down to earth. He told me that he'd already given a statement to the police. That basically he knew nothing. He'd never met Beverly. They'd only talked once by phone. But if I *had to* talk to him, he'd be around this evening.

I couldn't talk to Mike Taylor or even think about real food, until I washed the crust off my body. I headed for a long, hot shower.

With my thick hair wrapped in a towel, I slipped on my same jeans, but sniffed my tee shirt and found it unacceptable. Without Chad's array of flannel shirts at my disposal, I didn't know what to wear, so I paraded around with my chest bare and talked to Lola. "My little stumpy tail. What is your person going to eat?"

Lola positioned herself at the entrance to the hallway, what amounted to the center of the tiny house, so no matter where I traipsed, she simply had to turn her head to see me. Before she had been shot, Lola had possessed a long, fat tail, a reliable compass of her moods—straight up if she were happy or whacking against the wooden floor if she were annoyed. I missed that tail. I imagined she did, too.

Slowly I made decisions. First, my Shakespeare Santa Cruz sweatshirt. People might think I had some culture. The front showed a torso of Shakespeare in a Superman costume. Shakespeare Santa Cruz had been told that they couldn't use the Superman logo and had changed the image. So, my shirt was a collector's item even though the cotton was worn soft as fleece.

Next, Tortilla Flats, a little restaurant in downtown Soquel. It was charmingly decorated, but reasonably priced, and had a counter where single people could eat without having to pretend that everything was okay as they sat at a lonely table with a book.

Lastly, I'd see Mike Taylor that evening if he were available.

# CHAPTER 17

My first impression of Mike Taylor was that he could have strangled Beverly about as easily as most of us could squeeze a lime. Muscles stacked on muscles. They bulged against the hula girls on his Hawaiian shirt so they no longer swayed. I wondered if Mike Taylor could still bend down and tie his shoes. He wore Docksides when he entered Tortilla Flats.

He sat on a stool beside me. I immediately felt warm, probably because he blocked the draft from the door. With sandy hair and a tattoo that surely predated tattoo mania crawling up his freckled arm, he wasn't my type.

"Thanks for coming."

"I came for Cheryl's dessert." He caught the eye of the waitress. "Let me have a piece of that mango cheesecake. The biggest one."

He ordered like a drill sergeant.

I wanted one more bite of Santa Fe enchilada before we got down to business, but I'd barely started chewing when Mike Taylor said, "So what else can I tell you?"

"What did you and Beverly talk about on the phone?"

"Beverly had my number from her cousin and knew what I wanted, so we were direct with each other."

"What was it you wanted?"

The waitress slid his cheesecake onto the counter. "Big enough?"

"Thanks, sweetheart." He swiveled his head toward me. "You know what? Since I never met the woman and therefore didn't kill her, I don't think what we discussed is any of your business." He consumed a fourth of his cheesecake in one bite.

I looked around the small restaurant, completely full on this Saturday night. I wondered if any other diners were discussing sex and murder over their rice and beans.

"Is that what you told the police?"

"That's exactly what I told them. See I work at Spa Fitness on Forty-first Avenue and that night I had the late shift. After work, a couple of us went out. I was surrounded by people until the wee hours."

"Where did you go?"

"The Blue Lagoon."

That seemed like an odd choice for a he-man like Mike Taylor. The Blue Lagoon was a hopping nightclub, but it had a gay edge to it.

"Where do you work at the Spa?"

"On the exercise floor."

"Old building or new one?

"Old."

"Why didn't you hook up with Beverly? Wasn't she your type?"

He took another bite of cheesecake. He seemed irritated to be questioned, but securely innocent. I liked that he wanted to keep his sex life private. Refreshing in this age of Jerry Springer.

"Beverly sounded great. She was easy to talk to," he said. "Exactly my type."

"But?"

"She wanted money."

# CHAPTER 18

At home I had a phone message from my mom. Her voice was a whisper. "I think he knows about the envelope." There was a long pause. "I guess there's nothing you can do about that. I'll talk to you tomorrow." She hung up without saying goodbye. Again.

I sat on the edge of my bed and felt bad for a minute. How could Klaus Holthuis possibly know my mom had snooped in his mail? She was being paranoid. On the other hand, she wouldn't be in this position if it weren't for me.

Now that I'd put my mother through this trouble, I wasn't even sure what I'd do with the social security number. I could get a credit report with it, but my mom didn't need to know if Klaus Holthuis were financially responsible. I wasn't sure what she needed to know. Probably that she was safe and secure in her new home, something no one could assure her.

I could check if Klaus Holthuis had a criminal record. Since he was a university professor, I doubted it. He'd worked at Humboldt State, so if he'd lived in the area, any recent court documents regarding him would be in Eureka. The drive would take a whole day, and nothing drew me to my home turf. I still had relatives and a few high school friends in Humboldt County, but my hometown of Ferndale was one square mile of boredom surrounded by dairy farms. Despite the City Council's efforts to make the spruced-up Victorians a tourist destination, they couldn't change the overcast weather that blanketed the area like a metaphor for the depressed economy.

I dismissed the idea of driving to Eureka. I had a case

here to investigate. I carried the phone from the bedroom to my office, kicking the cord out of the way. On my last case, I'd dropped my phone on the floor when diving for cover. It had never worked right after that, so now I had a shiny white one with more buttons than I knew how to use. I steeled myself for the call I needed to make. He picked up on the second ring.

"Hi Uncle Teddy."

"By golly, Carol. I haven't heard from you in a coon's age."

*And you won't again until hell freezes or I need a favor.*

"How's your mom doing down there, Carol? Is she adjusting okay?"

*As if you care.*

Uncle Teddy was my mom's baby brother, born long after her and her older brother Beanie. Uncle Beanie was a cigar-chomping, skirt-chasing, gun-toting Republican, but my mom said the same things about him that she said about me, so we'd been allies.

On the other hand, Teddy was an anemic whiner, a spoiled autumn child, overly dependent on Uncle Beanie's generous salary to Teddy's wife.

"Mom's great, but she wants me to investigate one of her neighbors." I didn't say that she'd hired me. Uncle Teddy would have been too interested in the money she was paying. I glossed over the situation but asked if he'd be willing to stop by the Criminal Division of the Court Clerk's Office when he drove his wife to work in Eureka.

"Shoot, I'm going to the Home Depot tomorrow. I could check then."

"Tomorrow's Sunday."

"Not a problem. You remember Marie Clark?"

I pictured a woman with bird legs, one you knew occupied a regular seat at the end of a bar, her face prematurely desiccated from cigarette smoke and alcohol. "I think so."

"She's in charge there. We went to school together."

"I wouldn't go to any great lengths." I imagined Marie

Clark needed her beauty rest on a Sunday morning. Hopefully, Uncle Teddy would pump her full of stout black coffee before he asked for her help.

"I doubt that you will find anything," I said. "This guy's a professor." With Marie Clark as our helpmate, I felt pessimistic they'd find a record even if it existed. "But it might ease mom's anxiety if there are no cases featuring the State of California vs. Klaus Holthuis."

"Righto. I should be able to do that tomorrow. Give me a call."

It was so typical that he didn't offer to call me. With my uncles, I didn't give a rat's ass about politics. I had preferred the generous heart beating in my conservative Uncle Beanie to the penny-pinching whine in liberal Uncle Teddy's chest.

I dutifully asked after his wife and his son Brandon.

Brandon was getting all A's and Doreen was planning the family's trip to Paris.

Teddy sounded less than thrilled, probably because a trip to Paris would cost money.

After the call, I typed notes into my Beverly homicide file. I reread what I had. Nothing. I labeled a manila folder for the case and clipped into it the photos I'd gotten from Suzanne, one of Beverly fully dressed and leaning against the trunk of a Monterey pine. It was close up and clear, a good shot should I decide to canvas, a task too painful to consider.

The other two photos were of Beverly's male friends, the dead one Jim, and another one Pete. Suzanne knew Pete because he owned a carpet cleaning business and had been cleaning her carpets and her parents' carpets for years. She didn't consider him a suspect, but would bring his business card to work tomorrow, anyway.

I read and clipped the article from the morning paper. No suspects. No arrests. Just ongoing investigation, a photo of Beverly, and an appeal to the public. Just as David had deduced, she'd last been seen on Wednesday night in the Catalyst.

According to a witness, she'd been with a "young woman with light hair and a great bod." One witness thought he'd seen her on the sidewalk with a middle-aged white male. The police had obviously done some canvassing and were many steps ahead of me. I felt a familiar stab of guilt for taking Suzanne's money.

I copied Annie's phone number from the cocktail napkin to the inside of the folder and looked at my computer clock. Only nine. I punched the numbers on the phone.

Annie chirped hello. I reminded her of how we'd met and asked if I could interview her the next day.

"Are you a reporter?" she asked excitedly.

"A private investigator." I *was* an investigator, hired privately. I simply didn't have a license.

"That's cool, too. What are you investigating?"

"Have you heard about the death of Beverly Levandowsky?"

"Is she the woman they found on the levee?"

*Ding dong. Is anyone home?* This girl must actively avoid the local news.

"David Shapiro was the one who discovered the body."

"Really?" she shrieked. "I can't believe he didn't tell me. That loser. Is that why you want to interview me? To talk about David?" She sounded disappointed.

"Actually I think you knew the woman who was killed?"

"Really? I did? What did you say her name was?"

"Beverly Levandowsky."

"Beverly Leaden Down Ski? I don't think so. What did she look like?"

I started to describe Beverly. The blonde hair probably made blonder by a bottle. The big bosom and the outgoing personality.

"So far she sounds like my mother," Annie giggled.

"Did you ever pose nude with your mother?"

Now the girl laughed. The sound was tinkling and infectious. "That's really a weird thing to ask. My friend Sky was asking me just the other day . . . ." Annie laughed uncontrollably and I wondered if she were high. "Sky asked where I'd draw the line. That, I think . . . ." She laughed again. "That is where I'd draw the line." Annie drew deep breaths to calm herself. "Oh, God. Sorry. I guess you're saying I know this woman from modeling?"

"Yes." I thought of the PussyTech webpage. "Maybe you knew her as Randi?"

"Oh my God. Randi? Randi's dead?"

# CHAPTER 19

Slow Gherkin, a popular local ska band, was playing at the Catalyst, and young people thronged the entrance. As I approached the crowd, a scalper flashed two tickets at me. I shook my head.

I used to love this place. I'd seen Van Morrison here. I didn't know if this end of downtown had actually deteriorated or if it was just me, getting old. At this point in my life, the scruffy group outside, the drafty cavernous interior, and the dirty bathrooms annoyed me.

Fortunately, one didn't need a ticket to sit in the lobby, a gracious, high-ceilinged room draped in ferns. On Fridays, the side of the lobby would be converted to a stage and a section would be cleared of tables. In the late afternoon, Wally's Swing World would play and folks from twenty to eighty would ballroom dance over the colorful tiles. There was a sweetness to the place then that still drew me. But this was Saturday.

People spilled into the lobby's bar, thinking they could get a beer more quickly than inside the dance hall. I would have loved a beer, but didn't feel like fighting my way through the layers of people. The crowd was only there to grab drinks and get back to the music, so I had my choice of table. I sat near the tall front windows, away from the hubbub of the bar.

Meeting here had been Annie's idea. I didn't see anything to be gained that I couldn't have learned over the phone. But, the girl had a heightened sense of drama. She'd been here with Randi *the night of the murder. I might have been the last person to see Randi . . . Beverly . . . alive.*

No, I'd thought sarcastically, that had been the murderer.

But, Annie was the most important lead to date. The police had not yet located her. If I wanted every crumb of information she had to offer, I had to play along.

I hung my leather jacket over the wooden chair and pushed up the sleeves of my black shirt, trying to look casual and comfortable as a woman sitting alone. After ten years with a partner, the feeling did not come naturally. I didn't have to feign nonchalance for long.

Annie strolled in, her big shoes clomping on the tile, weighing down thin legs protruding from a black leather mini skirt. Beadwork scrolled along the shoulders of a white button-up sweater. She'd ratted her blond hair and applied frosty lipstick for a Sixties look.

"I dressed exactly like I was Wednesday." She slid onto a chair and sedately parked a lunch-pail purse and her cell phone on the table.

"Want a beer?" I asked.

"Sure."

Something made me hesitate. Perhaps a slight blush under the glitter on her cheeks. "How old are you?"

"Twenty."

"Were you drinking on Wednesday?"

She blushed again. She wore glitter at the top of her chest, too.

"I don't care that you're not twenty-one," I said. "I'm not a police officer."

"Sloe gin fizzes."

"How many?"

She stuck out her frosty lips like a pouting child. She'd clearly intended to be not only the star actress, but also the director of this scene.

"I guess I was on my third."

"When . . . ?"

Her green eyes studied me. She clearly had no idea what I was fishing for.

"What happened when you were on your third drink?"

"Randi said she was going to call for a cab to take me home."

"Did she do that?"

"No." Annie spun her phone on the table. "Actually that really pissed me off."

"Why? I mean, after three sloe gin fizzes, I'd be pretty looped. It seems like she was watching out for you."

"Sure. But I didn't want to go home. We'd been out partying like girlfriends, and then she started tripping, acting like my mom." Annie still sounded peeved at Beverly, as though it hadn't completely sunk in that Beverly was dead.

"Did Beverly buy you your drinks?"

Her eyes narrowed. "I paid for them."

"But she ordered them."

She regarded me suspiciously. Was I trying to incriminate her friend Randi? Was I trying to remind her that she was a child?

"So you two were partying. What was the occasion? Anything special?"

"Randi . . . Beverly . . . I can't get used to that name. I'm just going to call her Randi, okay?"

I nodded. Again it struck me that Annie did not fully grasp Beverly's death. She was more excited to be part of a drama than shocked or saddened by loss.

"Randi just asked me if I wanted to go. We'd had a shoot that day for a guy named Cole."

"Cole of PussyTech fame?" I wondered if Annie knew what she was getting into.

"Yeah," she said. "You know him?"

"I've met him. What kind of work did you do?"

"Just the usual cheesecake stuff. He pays really well."

"Were the photos for his webpage?"

She rearranged her lunch-pail purse, putting it in a

perpendicular position to where it had formerly rested. "I suppose so."

She snapped the latch of the purse and stared out the window. My curiosity wanted to lead me into the quagmire of Annie's motivations for doing that kind of work. In a town that mostly offered minimum-wage jobs for college students, money was no doubt a factor.

But, Annie's delicate chin was already thrust out, and I was not advancing my collection of data about Beverly. I had to keep myself focused on the purpose of this interview. Cole hadn't mentioned that he'd seen Beverly on the day of her murder. "Did anything strange happen at that shoot?"

"Cole and Randi got into an argument."

"About what?"

"I'm not sure. I was in the bathroom. It sounded like it was about money. I got the impression Cole was leaving and Randi wanted him to pay her before he took off. They stopped when I came out."

"On a scale of one to ten, how angry did they seem?"

"I don't know." Annie shrugged. "About a six. Cole kissed Randi on the cheek when we left. She said, 'Bye, Mr. Cheap Ass,' but she didn't knee him in the crotch or anything. Overall, Randi was in a good mood. She seemed excited about something."

"So did you drive yourself . . . ?"

Annie raised her chin, the typical twenty-something greeting and smiled slightly. "There's my teacher," she said.

I twisted around to look toward the bar.

She hissed at me. "Geez, could you be less obvious?"

I snapped my head back around, thoroughly chagrined.

"He's so fine," she purred. "When you turn around this time, slowly, like you're just thinking about a beer, look to nine o'clock. He's the tall blond."

I rotated my head discreetly.

"That's enough," Annie whispered fiercely. "Don't stare."

I turned back to her. "I didn't even see him."

She rolled her eyes and chuckled. "You are *the worst.*" She turned her black lunch-pail purse. "This is pointing straight at him. Come over here like you're giving me something and then look up just where this is pointing."

Feeling like a dunce, I did as directed. I followed the line of the purse straight into the eyes of Klaus Holthuis.

# CHAPTER 20

Klaus waggled his fingers and sauntered toward us, bottle of beer in hand, clean-cut and collegial, relaxed and handsome. I ducked back onto my seat. He towered over us.

"What is it you Americans say? It's a small world." He beamed at his command of idioms. If he lived long in the same building with my mother, he'd have an opportunity to master them all.

In spite of her imagined superiority in the realm of flirtation, Annie gaped. "Do you two know each other?"

"Klaus lives in the same building as my mother."

Klaus stood, waiting like a gentleman for us to invite him to sit. I understood my reluctance. I felt guilty about the way my mom and I were prying into his life. If he had some intimation my mom had opened his mail, I didn't want to confirm it with my open-book face. On the other hand, Annie's reluctance was baffling. She clearly had a crush on the professor and wasn't bashful. Or at least, I assumed she wasn't since she took off her clothes for a living.

"Your mom tells me that you're buying a house, Carol," Klaus said.

His statement surprised me. But if my mom had been backed into a conversational corner, my attempt to buy a house might have seemed like a safe topic. "Yes. It belonged to me and my husband, but now we're divorced. I'm trying to buy him out."

"I'd like to buy here," he said. "Where is your house located?"

As he stood awkwardly at our table, we chatted about real estate.

Annie was no help at all. She acted like a shy schoolgirl, studying the table.

Finally, Klaus said, "If you will excuse me, I shall return to the music. This band is fabulous." He quirked a brow. "Perhaps you will join me."

"We don't have tickets," Annie said.

He gave her a brief, paternal smile and said something in German. The aggressive, guttural sound reminded me of why I'd stuck to Spanish.

As Klaus strolled away, drinking his beer, I asked, "Don't you like him?"

"You can't act too eager," she said condescendingly.

"What did he say?"

"That he'd see me later."

"In class?"

She shrugged. "I suppose."

"What possessed you to take German?"

"International business. That's what I'm studying. I'm learning Chinese, too."

*Holy shit.* My eyes refocused, trying to see the business student under the glitter. I was impressed, but the hour was late and I was weary. "I just have a couple more questions. How *did* you get home Wednesday night?"

"I ran into my housemate Shawn and he gave me a lift. I came back for my car on Thursday."

"Did you see Beverly meet anyone?"

"No. But I think she was going to and that's why she wanted to get rid of me."

# CHAPTER 21

I plodded toward my car in a lot behind the Catalyst. The day had been an exhausting, emotional roller coaster and the chat with Annie had been irritatingly unproductive. I'd advised her to talk to the Santa Cruz homicide detectives as soon as possible and we'd arranged to meet the next afternoon for follow up. My best questions often popped into my brain the minute I left an interview. But not this time.

Crossing my arms, I huddled against the cold of the night, keys in hand, staying alert. I parked in the lot because it was free, but it was too dark to be safe. When I touched my car door handle, I received a flicker of inspiration.

I cut back across the side street and headed toward the Blue Lagoon. This was Saturday night, late enough for Mike Taylor to be off work, and people had their regular haunts.

House music thrummed onto the sidewalk, pulsing in my shoes. A bouncer the size of a small elephant stood outside the door.

"Five dollars," he said.

The music was too loud and I was too cold to protest.

The Blue Lagoon was a deep, narrow club with enough people pressed inside to violate any fire code.

I put out my hands as though I were going to dive into a pool. "Excuse me!" I shouted at two transvestites blocking my way.

The place smelled like old beer and vomit with a thin overlay of disinfectant. Dim lights snaked down from the dark ceiling. The best light glowed from the aquarium that divided the bar from the minuscule dance floor in the back.

I wedged by the D.J.'s booth into the strobbing light. I stepped up onto a built-in bench, wedging my hightops between a seated couple in leather pants and ripped t-shirts. "Excuse me!" They looked alike, peroxided hair plastered with sweat to shiny faces. "I'm trying to spot someone on the dance floor."

They were oblivious. Drugged or maybe just catching their breaths.

In the fractured light, I caught kaleidoscope images. A muscled arm. Slim gyrating hips. A jerk of sandy hair. Mike Taylor was dancing with a small, elegant black man.

Not detecting my own brother's sexual orientation had permanently humbled me about my ability to identify a gay person. But then, who wouldn't have been confused? Mike had said Beverly was perfect; he just didn't want to pay for her services. Perhaps he defied a sexual label.

I hopped off the bench, lifted my arms, and wiggled my hips onto the dance floor. I bumped and grinded and strategically flailed my arms.

Mike Taylor knew in a second that I wasn't out clubbing on a Saturday night. His reaction was swift and unequivocal. He grabbed my arm and propelled us both through the crowd.

No one missed a beat. You didn't come to a place like this on a Saturday night if you minded being jostled and bumped.

Mike Taylor steered me to the entrance. I felt like a puppy unceremoniously deposited on the sidewalk. All he would have had to add was *bad girl*.

Instead he said, "I thought I made it clear I like my privacy."

"Don't let this twit back in," he said to the elephant. "She's a private eye."

He disappeared past the two transvestites. They were still gossiping near the entrance with exaggerated, theatrical gestures.

I might have felt humiliated if I weren't basking in the glow of having been conferred the status of a real investigator. "If I can't go in, I think I should get a refund," I said to the elephant.

He shrugged indifferently, peeled a five-dollar bill from a huge roll and slapped it into my palm. "Have a lovely evening."

I started toward my Ghia, anxious to go home, chastising myself for that little foray. What exactly had I accomplished?

I stopped outside Streetlight Records and rummaged in my pocket for my keys. Lower Pacific was the sleazy end of the downtown mall. I wanted to have my keys out and ready. The temperature felt as though it had dropped another five degrees. I hustled toward the parking lot, searching another pocket.

A force like a tornado picked me up and used my own momentum to slam my head into a wooden fence. A strong hand braced my neck, pinning my face forward. I couldn't see anything.

A powerful body leaned into me. His legs straddled mine so that I couldn't kick. An arm restrained my torso. The hand slithered to the front of my neck. The cool impersonal touch was familiar. Silky. The hand of a doctor. A hand in latex gloves.

I twisted with all my strength to the left, managing an elbow into his ribs.

He didn't even grunt.

I scrunched my shoulders to protect my neck, but the fingers expertly found my windpipe. They squeezed. A strangling cough choked up my throat. My head spun. The darkness grew darker. My knees weakened.

"Would you like something to enhance your experience?" a young voice asked.

I slid down the fence and collapsed on the asphalt.

The two voices above me sounded like children, a boy and a girl. "I thought he was kissing her neck," the boy said defensively.

"He's probably the guy who killed the woman on the levee," the girl whispered. She touched my neck with cold, trembling fingers. "Did you get a look at him?"

"So what if I did? I can't call the cops," the boy said. "I'm carrying enough shit for an army. I can hear them now, 'And what were you doing back there, Sonny Boy?'"

"We can't leave her. That dude might come back and kill her."

I pushed to my hands and knees with a painful cough. "I'm okay."

They jumped and fled, the girl in bare feet. Her long skirt whirled up the scent of sandalwood and jewelry jangled on her ankles.

I stumbled to my Ghia and made it safely home where I sat with an ice pack to the lump on my forehead, pecking with one finger to update my files.

*Got attacked.* I was pumped full of adrenaline and oddly calm. I noted the time and place. The latex gloves. But I didn't have much. The man was strong and I would have guessed taller than I was.

Mike Taylor? How would he have gotten to the lot before me? Was there a back way out of the Blue Lagoon? Probably. And he seemed chummy with the people in charge.

The man hadn't spoken. But I had smelled something. Also medicinal. Adding to the association with a doctor's office. Antiseptic. Mouthwash?

Was the girl right? Was my attacker the levee killer? Why would a killer use mouthwash? Was it part of a sick, courtly love?

Or maybe the guy was thinking about kissing someone else. I flashed on Mike Taylor's hot dance partner.

I sent an e-mail to Cole. I imagined him in black chaps on his Harley, the modern Easy Rider, a laptop strapped to the bitch seat, rather than drugs in the gas tank.

In the e-mail, I asked about his shoot with Beverly and Annie. Had he and Beverly argued? About what? Did he know what Bev was up to that day?

He'd failed to mention he'd seen Beverly on the day of the murder, but that didn't surprise me. I'd expect a pornographer to avoid the attention of an investigation. I was surprised that he'd even given me his contact info.

I didn't expect a reply. And even if Cole did respond, he

could take his time composing a lie. No body language would betray him.

If I hadn't known that Eldon was overwhelmed with Beverly's loss and the police investigation, I would have called in sick. Instead, I dug out a turtleneck to wear the next day. It should cover the bruises appearing on my neck. At least with the chaos, Eldon didn't have time to organize splitting my job into two jobs.

I climbed into bed and Lola jumped up beside me. Trying to concoct creative lies to explain the bump on my forehead, I finally fell asleep.

The next morning, as I pulled dough from my fingers, I thought testily that I didn't understand the allure of scones. They were nothing but glorified baking powder biscuits. The same thing you got at Kentucky Fried.

Of course, unlike baking powder biscuits, scones contained eggs and at Archibald's we added fresh blueberries and my secret ingredient of lemon zest. And we served the finished product with clotted cream.

I was sniffing the air for the doneness of the scones when I smelled Suzanne. Or to be more accurate, Hamad.

I bowed down to her. "Long live Kuwait. Where George Bush is revered and you can buy all the fast food you want, but no beer to go with it." The speech scratched up through my sore throat and struggled out.

Although her face no longer looked raw from tears, Suzanne didn't smile. "At least people don't get strangled there." Her white chef's smock washed out her face color, and for a second Suzanne seemed like a sibyl, aware of last night's events. Then I realized she was referring to Beverly.

I donned my oven mitts and turned away from her to the scones. "Unless they're servants. Then it's amazing if the death is reported."

"You're making that up."

I decided to allow Suzanne her romantic illusions for the moment. I backed one heavy tray from the oven and stepped sideways to slide it onto the cooling racks. I preferred not to have company when I did this job to avoid any accidental branding.

"Why's your voice so hoarse?" she asked my back.

"Sore throat."

Suzanne slapped a business card for Galvan's Carpet Cleaning onto the stainless steel table. "I don't know why you don't like Hamad," she pouted. "You haven't even met him."

"I just don't want some guy to whisk away my friend to a place where women can't even vote."

"The cool thing about Kuwait is you can get on a plane and in a few hours be in Greece or India or Africa."

I extracted another tray and sighed. Anyone who could begin a sentence with *The cool thing about Kuwait* was hopeless. "Come here, Suzanne."

She took three obedient steps across the room.

"Stand in front of the oven."

She did.

I opened the door. "That's Kuwait."

She backed away. "They have air conditioning."

She was smitten. Logic had flown the coop and probably wouldn't return until the heat from the Kuwaiti tarmac scalded her ankles.

"It's not like I'd be moving there."

She twirled the business card while I finished transferring the trays.

"I don't think it's even worth interviewing Pete Galvan," she said, changing the subject.

"The bad thing about hiring me is you don't get to decide what's worth investigating. That's my job."

"Okay. Sorry."

With this newfound passivity, she'd fit right in with the Kuwaiti women. She didn't even notice the quarter-sized blue bump on my forehead. I'd strategically arranged some tendrils of hair, but I hadn't expected them to fool my best friend.

"Look, Suzanne. I had a thought last night. Has anyone checked the lockers?"

"Why would they?"

That was a legitimate question. Usually employees locked up their personal effects only during their shifts. Whatever Beverly had with her at work that day, she would, presumably, have taken with her.

"Well, I've finally met the infamous Mike Taylor." I didn't plan to alarm her with a single detail of the subsequent attack. "He has an alibi for Wednesday night. He could be lying, but it's an easy story to check. Bev had a rendezvous with someone."

I glossed over the meeting with Annie, too, not wanting to stir false hope that I was hot on the trail of the killer. Or worse yet, stir fear that the killer was hot on my trail. Better to have Suzanne think it was a mistake to hire me.

"I don't think she just bumped into her killer," I said. "I think they had a date. So where's the phone number or the jotted name or the notation of the time? Not in her condo."

"Probably in her purse and the guy took it along with the money."

"That's likely."

Still Suzanne's brown eyes pulsed with excitement. "Let's go look."

"Let's do an official check out for break." With Eldon busy in the Employees Dining Room, we had more freedom of movement than usual. But I didn't want to put Eldon in a position where he should write me up, but wouldn't for fear I'd gossip about him.

The locker room was a unisex affair with a screened section for each sex. The sidewalls had rows of a dozen over and under lockers, most of them dangling standard black combination locks. In the most unobtrusive spot, bottom locker on the end, Suzanne said, "You're right, Carol. This is her lock."

I knelt beside her. "How can you tell?"

"The dot of red nail polish in the center. Beverly did that so she could tell her lock from the others."

"Do you know her combination?"

"No."

"We'll have to get someone to cut the lock."

"You could ask Eldon," she said.

"I can't ask him. He expects me to be snooping around. If I ask, he'll insist that the police be called."

"I can't do it. Since the herpes story, we hardly talk."

"You have to do it."

"He'll still want to call the police."

"Tell him it's your locker and you forgot the combination."

Suzanne fiddled with the lock. "He won't believe that."

"Of course he will. From you, people believe the check's in the mail."

"What am I going to tell him? Why do I need to get into my locker?"

I put my finger to my lips. She quieted. "It's been my experience that when a woman says she needs to get into her personal stuff, most guys don't ask why."

She nodded. We left the locker room and Suzanne headed down the hall to the Employees Dining Room. I returned to the bakery, hot and redolent with blueberry and lemon.

I was halfway up to my elbows in bread dough when Suzanne appeared in the doorway. Her eyes jumped nervously.

"What did you find?"

"All kinds of stuff. Lotion and deodorant and underwear. A veritable home away from home. But this is what you want to see." She pulled a copy of *Good Times*, a Santa Cruz weekly, from behind her smock. A hole was torn in the relationship ads.

# CHAPTER 22

The *Good Times* office was over the Santa Cruz Pacific Cookie Company and the fragrance of chocolate chip cookies followed me up the concrete stairs.

The small front reception area was empty so I flagged a girl from the back who looked as though she hadn't combed her hair any time recently. Her thong sandals slapped across the floor. She arrived at the counter and stared at me until I asked if there might be a copy of last week's *Good Times* that I could have. She fetched the paper, wordlessly slid it across the counter, and had no response to my thank you. Typical enthusiasm among young workers in Santa Cruz.

I descended the stairs, passed under the maroon awnings, and situated myself on a sidewalk bench before I opened the paper. I'd left the original with Suzanne to give to the police, but the location of the hole was burned into my brain. On the back side had been Risa's Stars, the astrology column.

"Maybe she tore out the Sagittarius forecast," Suzanne had said. "She *was* a Sagittarius."

I was doubtful.

"Why would she answer a relationship ad? I had to push her to check out Mike," Suzanne had persisted. "Guys were falling all over her."

"That's the same thing I wondered about you," I said.

Now I quickly skimmed the page. The torn-out section had been big enough to encompass three personal ads, but I knew which one had fascinated Beverly the moment I saw it. I circled it in black ink.

*Mr. Wrong.*

# CHAPTER 23

The nearest available private phone was at my mom's. I needed to see her anyway about Klaus Holthuis. First I saw the guy at the Catalyst. Then someone threw me into a fence. While Mike Taylor topped my list of suspicious brutes, I couldn't rule out Klaus. He'd seemed smooth and flirtatious. But if my mom was right and he suspected we'd gone through his mail, he had a reason to be pissed. Although trying to strangle me seemed like an overreaction, to say the least.

Normally I would have hoofed the half mile from the Pacific Cookie Company to Hinds House, especially since I'd found a free parking space and it was against my principles to pay to park. But today anxiety prickled my skin.

Besides following up on this ad, I needed to calm my mom, to ask Annie more questions about the night of the murder, and to check out Pete, the carpet cleaner. So I drove closer to Hinds House and wasted as much time circling the block as it would have taken to walk. Finally, a young woman pranced down the steps of Hinds House, jumped into an old blue Mustang convertible, and roared away. I pulled into the spot not more than twenty feet from the steps. *God is smiling on me.*

The door to the Victorian was open. Chris Isaak sang mournfully. The front entry and side rooms teemed with people.

It was Sunday. All those grad students and professors were home and having a party.

Klaus Holthuis ambushed me from the parlor. "Ah. The delightful Carol Sabala. We meet again so soon."

Even as the memory of being pitched into a fence throbbed in my forehead, I felt like crawling under the huge display of gladiolus. I was stinky from work and dusted with flour like a dry noodle. Klaus had abandoned two women on the velveteen sofa. They studied me with clear envy as he clasped my hand and raised it to his lips. "Where's your mother?" he asked. "She seems to be avoiding us. Me, in particular, I think."

"She's not a party animal."

He laughed as though I'd been terribly witty. But I wondered how my reserved mom was dealing with the situation.

About thirty people milled in the two rooms. Munching crackers and sipping wine, they came and went from the back kitchen.

"What do you have under your arm?"

"Just a *Good Times*." Unfortunately turned and folded to display the circled ad which Klaus Holthuis bent over and twisted his head to read.

He straightened and wiggled his golden eyebrows at me. "Doing a little shopping, Carol?"

My face felt as hot as new bread. Partly because a handsome man with an accent was teasing me, but mainly because he'd exposed me as a careless sleuth, recklessly displaying newfound evidence.

"Mr. Wrong," he said. "Sounds like me."

"Is my mom upstairs?"

He shrugged. "Why don't you stay for the party? Try to persuade your mother to join us."

I *should* spend some time chatting up the professor, gathering information for my mom. Last night he'd adeptly kept the conversation focused on me and where I lived, when I should have been finding out about him. I was beginning to understand why becoming a private investigator required so many training hours. I was obviously a novice. If I had learned exactly where he'd lived in Northern California, or where he'd lived before that, I'd have a clearer idea of which court records to scan. I'd had the perfect conversational entry, and I'd blown it.

"I'll catch you later." I left Klaus repeating this idiom to himself and headed for the steps.

With stabs of pain shooting into the bottoms of my knees, I banged on my mom's door. Patellar tendonitis, called jumper's knee, had put an end to my volleyball playing. Normally, as long as I didn't jump, I was fine, but my knees didn't appreciate bounding up two flights of steps, either.

My mother opened her door and sniffed. "Well this is a fine kettle of fish."

"Hi, mom. Glad to see you, too."

She waved me into her room and made a production of scouting around the landing, locking the door and closing the window above it.

"So what's going on, mom? You know when you leave a message, you could say goodbye."

"Why should I say goodbye to a machine?"

I sighed, sat in a wicker chair and massaged my knees.

"What happened to your forehead?"

"Ran into a wall."

The same radar that had seen through my lame attempt to hide the bump with my hair, also informed my mom that she wouldn't get anything more out of me. She sat on the bed and managed to look bleak in spite of her aqua warm-up suit. "That man—"

"Klaus Holthuis?"

Her expression said *Did I unleash this idiot into the world?*

"Yes," she said with world-weary patience. "Klaus Holthuis. Yesterday he saw me by the mailboxes right after I'd returned his insurance letter."

"That doesn't sound so bad."

"I didn't think it was so bad, either. He didn't have any mail, but there were letters in some other boxes. But then I saw mine was empty and I realized the mail hadn't come. I guess some people just aren't very diligent about collecting their mail. Anyway, I couldn't take the envelope out because he was there. Then he came over and said, 'Hi, Bea, waiting for the mailman?' like I was some lonely old lady he felt sorry for. Of course he saw the envelope that shouldn't have been there."

"And?"

"And nothing. He took out the envelope and I walked away."

I regretted involving my mother in this mess, especially since I had absolutely nothing to show for her worry and paranoia. "If he's a normal person, he will assume something normal happened. Like his letter had been mixed with someone else's mail."

"Like mine. I should have said it was mixed with mine."

I could see where I'd inherited my tendency to beat myself up.

"Now he's watching me," she mourned. "And he could be that levee murderer."

I wanted to reassure her that if Klaus were a murderer, the safest person she could be was his neighbor. But that sounded too flip for the woman on the bed, who suddenly wasn't my mother, but simply an old woman with an incipient dowager's hump and frightened eyes.

"What have you found out about him?" she asked.

"I'm looking into the court records in Eureka," I exaggerated, "but since he's a professor, I doubt I'll discover anything."

"Look, Carol, if you want the ten thousand dollars, you will have to earn it. I'm not going to *give* it to you."

The vulnerable old woman was my aggravating mother again. "I never asked you for the money."

"And you probably never would because you're stubborn, Carol. You were so stubborn you refused to be born . . . ."

I tuned out the story of my mom's record-breaking labor. When she wound down, I simply said, "It's true. I'm stubborn. Could I use your phone?"

She pointed at it.

When I called the 900 number for the relationship ads and punched in the mailbox number for Mr. Wrong, I received the recorded message, "Sorry. The mailbox number you've entered is not a valid number."

God wasn't smiling on me. He was having his usual ping-pong tournament.

# CHAPTER 24

Make that a hockey tournament with me as the puck. When I returned to the street, the front tire of my Ghia was completely flat. *Anything that can go wrong, will go wrong.* Murphy's Law. One of my mother's favorites.

Like most Ghia owners, I had a cultish fondness for my car, the design Italian, by Ghia of Turin, the hand-welded seams by Karmann of Osnabrück. Now she was like a racehorse who'd pulled up lame. I patted her flank.

When I reentered the party zone, one of the women from the couch bee-lined toward me. She had porcelain skin and blue eyes, and would have been attractive if she hadn't looked so conservative, dressed in a peach twin set and her brown hair fried from too much perming. "Have you seen Klaus?" she asked. "He asked to use my car and disappeared on us."

"Maybe he went for beer."

"Oh no," she said seriously, "we have a whole keg."

"Do you live here?"

She stepped back and frowned. "I beg your pardon."

"I have a flat tire and wondered if you had access to a phone that's closer than my mom's on the third floor."

"I work with Klaus at the university," she said brusquely.

Even though I had a flat tire to fix, this woman would be a good person to interview at some point. "What's your name?"

The wide spaced eyes flicked up and down. "Alice Miller," she said reluctantly. "And you are . . . ?"

"Carol Sabala."

Alice's good manners demanded that she shake, although

she took my hand as though it were a banana slug.

I excused myself and took the steps two at a time until my knees rebelled. At my mom's door, the lurid St. Francis extended his blue hands in greeting. I knocked and my mom called out, "Who's there?" Her voice quavered and I felt guilty again for not taking her fear more seriously. Whether a threat was real or imagined, the fear was the same.

"It's me."

She opened the door, her eyes spitting fire, but clearly relieved it was me. "What's wrong?"

"Flat tire."

"Do you need to call Triple A?"

"No." To save money, I'd quit the service. "I just have to call someone I was going to meet to tell her I'll be late."

"Do you need some help?" She looked certain I'd refuse. Too damned stubborn.

I doubted my mom could be of much help except as moral support, but right now some moral support seemed like an excellent idea. "That would be ducky."

While I called Annie, my mom took off her aqua warm-up jacket and put on an old flannel shirt.

I received a busy signal.

My mom stood in the corner and turned her back to me as she changed into some brown work pants. I kept my eyes averted. My mom's modesty, as much as anything, had been the reason she'd never acknowledged my brother Donald's sexual orientation. Even though she'd spent years up close and personal with people's oral cavities, she could barely talk about other orifices.

I punched redial. Still busy.

As we clomped down the stairs, my mom said, "You know your Great Uncle Toby was run over and killed while changing a tire."

*So much for moral support.* But I appreciated my mom standing between me and the traffic on Chestnut Street. It took five minutes and half a can of WD40 to get the lug nuts to budge.

The party people had grown used to me and didn't even turn as I trooped back through the foyer and climbed the stairs to call Annie again. The line remained busy. I was surprised that she didn't have call waiting.

My tendons injected pain below the knees as I walked back down the steps. I wished I had a cell phone, although I considered them public nuisances on par with dog shit. Like dogs, phones weren't the problem, but rather their self-absorbed owners. People who brought their phones to the theater, the restaurant, and the beach, people who interrupted the calming surge of the surf with, "Ooh, ick, you gotta be kidding" as though their puny dramas deserved equal billing with God's creation.

The world might be a better place if everyone were as private as my mother, who instead of standing and waiting for me as I'd commanded, was cranking the jack.

I shooed her away. "Your job is to make sure I'm not road kill like Uncle Toby."

She rolled the flat tire, inspecting each section, running her hand over the dirty surface. "I don't see any nail," she pronounced.

"It's an old tire."

"Someone might have let the air out."

"Why would anyone do that?"

"A prank."

That seemed like a prank from a different era. Like ringing doorbells and hiding.

"Maybe someone wanted to keep you here," she said.

"Oh, yeah, I'm just the life of a party." My fingers were black and grubby and my mood felt like a good match.

Mom crossed her arms over her plaid flannel shirt and turned to watch the traffic on Chestnut. I'd tightened the lug nuts before my mom deigned to speak again. "What I meant is the person may have wanted to keep you from getting to wherever you're going."

# CHAPTER 25

Pneumonia Flats on the west side of Santa Cruz was an area devoid of charm. The weather blighted flowers and the salty air rusted cars. The morning fog took much longer to burn off here than it did in the banana belt where I lived. With a rush of smugness, I became more determined than ever to buy the house from Chad.

Some folks loved this area because it was near the ocean. But it sat on a level cliff, so only those near the beach had a view, while everyone felt the presence of the Pacific. Dampness permeated the linoleum, the paint, and one's skin.

Annie lived in a part of Pneumonia Flats where back in the 1800's a massive, octagonal Tabernacle had stood with a road circling it. Plots surrounding the church had been sold to the faithful, giving Santa Cruz a neighborhood of confusing circular streets. Annie's street was a ray off a circle.

Her address led to a white stucco bungalow with sheets in the windows, a couch on the porch, and two old bicycles chained together. Grass and weeds came to my shins.

When I'd called Annie for the fourth time from the Hinds House, her phone had still been busy, but now silence enveloped the house. The white Cabriolet was not in the driveway that ended in the back at a dilapidated detached garage. I didn't see it parked on the street, either. I rang the bell, but no one answered. I knocked and tried to peek around the sheet curtains.

The place was deserted.

I sighed and sat on the steps for a moment to collect my thoughts, the first of which was that this day sucked. I was tired and powdered with flour. My knees hurt. I'd had that stupid flat tire and not one of my leads had panned out. Suzanne should fire me.

Since I'd talked to Annie at the Catalyst, I'd come up with a thousand questions I wanted to ask about the night of the murder. First and foremost, had Beverly mentioned the relationship ads. Had she kidded about Mr. Wrong?

I waited for ten minutes with the vague hope that Annie had popped out and would be right back. I idly looked under the worn welcome mat for a spare key. It wasn't there, but I found it soon enough under a clay pot growing a gray stem. Giving into a foreboding that nothing would work out for me today, I left the key untouched and went to my car to scrounge for a pen and a piece of paper.

When investigating, I preferred to leave my purse at home. I managed by cramming money in my pockets and carrying my driver's license in my car, but it was becoming clear that I'd have to organize myself better.

I wrote Annie a note on a blank strip torn from the edge of the *Good Times,* telling her to call me as soon as possible. I placed the edge under the mat.

I plopped on the steps again to ponder what to do next. I could interview Pete, the carpet cleaner. Since it was Sunday, I might be able to catch him at home. I could check on Mike Taylor's alibi, although it seemed doubtful that he would lie about working when it was so easy to check. And, it was improbable that he'd slipped away from the Spa unnoticed for a long enough period to drive downtown, sweet talk Beverly into a late night stroll along the levee, and choke her to death.

I considered going to the nearest gas station instead, to see if I needed a tire. I hadn't been able to see anything embedded in the rubber, either. My mom might be right. Maybe someone had deflated it.

I propped my elbows on my knees, cupped my chin in my hands, and watched a towhee hop around in the overgrown grass of Annie's yard. Keeping a watchful eye, its mate chirped periodically from the neighbor's liquid amber tree. Towhees weren't much to look at. Medium-sized brown birds with slightly rosy breasts, but I loved them for their touching loyalty to their partners.

My musing on partnerships led to thoughts of David Shapiro. A slightly queasy feeling burbled in the pit of my stomach. That was the guy I should talk to. He'd discovered the body. He knew Annie, who knew Beverly. He had even mentioned placing a relationship ad.

If I'd had a cell phone, I would have called him right then. I wanted to know if David Shapiro's ad said *Mr. Wrong*.

# CHAPTER 26

I didn't do any of the planned things first. Instead I stopped at Staff of Life and bought a heaping hand basket of organic lettuce, hormone-free milk, and granola made with ungenetically-altered grain. In the other hand I toted a six-pack of Sierra Nevada beer.

A guy with unnatural blonde dreadlocks to his waist rang up my groceries while he chatted about a movie to a girl with hennaed hair. Possibly she was the bagger.

At home the first order of business, before the butter even went in the refrigerator, was Her Royal Highness Lola. After I'd lavished HRH with enough pets, she spread eagled on her back. I'd once thought of this as the cute little otter pose, but in my current state of mind, Lola reminded me of a lewd woman.

I constructed myself a sandwich with three seed bread, smoked turkey breast, slices of Swiss cheese, Dijon mustard, sprouts, and tomato. I piled the thing like the Empire State Building and sat on the tiny brick landing in my backyard to eat. My jaw popped with each bite. Failure worked up quite an appetite.

The sun felt great and Lola strolled out to curl behind me. After eating, I indulged in a long, hot shower and changed into shorts and a man's white tee shirt. I went back into the sun to dry my hair. I slathered my body with vanilla scented lotion, filed my nails, and put on mascara. I'd be damned if I were going to run into another hunk while I was looking and feeling like a dry crust of bread.

Sufficiently fortified, I checked my e-mail. I had a message from Cole Thomas of PussyTech fame.

*Hello Cutie. I guess you've tracked down Annie. Of course I didn't tell you about the shoot. Why would I? I needed to get the hell out of Dodge before the fuzz asked me to stick around. I'm sorry as hell about Beverly, but Sturgis is the biggest event of the year for me. Me staying in Santa Cruz wouldn't help anything. I don't know who killed her. Wasn't me. Why would I? She's a gold mine. We did get into it that day over money—same old shit. I tried to explain to her that she was special, but bottom line, girls are a dime a dozen. Bev did seem amped. I think she was excited about meeting someone. Tell you the truth, I was a little jealous. But now, I am in the Black Hills and everything's copacetic. I expect the cops, or who knows, maybe you, to have this all wrapped up by the time I get back. —Cole*

*P.S. I'm always looking for new talent.*

His slimy ruthlessness oozed through the keyboard. I washed my hands and then called David Shapiro. No answer. Par for the day. I expected an outrageous message, but received the standard, *"I'm sorry that I missed your call . . . ."*

As I was identifying myself, he picked up the phone. Music blared in the background. "It's Nancy Drew!" he sang. "That's MC5." Raucous rock grew louder. "Like it?" He turned down the volume.

"It's hard to tell over the phone." I paced my small bedroom, six steps to the sliding glass door and six steps back.

"That's true," David Shapiro said. "You should come over. It's a beautiful afternoon. We could go on that bike ride."

This guy never got discouraged. "Are you doing a photo shoot?" I asked, remembering the deafening music that day with Annie. "Is Annie there?"

"The coast is clear. There are no other women present."

Sometimes a smooth segue back to one's purpose doesn't exist. I resorted to my mom's bluntness. "I called because I was curious what you put in your personal ad."

"You're not thinking about placing one, are you?"

"No."

He reflected a couple of seconds. "Don't worry," he said. "You meet all my criteria."

"I'll be the judge of that."

"I put that I was a professional Jewish male in search of a five-foot-eight woman with auburn hair in her late thirties. Interest in investigating a plus."

I sighed and sat on my bed. This guy was impossible.

"Okay," he relented. "I had a great ad. The standard sketch of me, and then *no big hair, New Agers, tie dye or Republicans.*"

I laughed, relieved he wasn't Mr. Wrong. "That was you?"

"You saw it?" he asked. "What did you think?"

"I have big hair. And how do you know I'm not a Republican?"

"Rush is right," he quipped.

I groaned, giving away my politics. "What about the big hair?"

"You're under the legal limit. You qualify."

*Qualify for what? To be strangled?*

"Did Annie ever talk about another model named Randi?"

"Why are we back to Annie? I thought we were talking about you."

"I thought you said interest in investigating is a plus." In my diminutive yard the Peruvian lilies were smashed in the center by Lola and the cosmos needed to be deadheaded.

"I take it back."

"Seriously, though, did she ever mention Randi?"

"Quid pro quo. Who's Randi?"

"Randi was one of Beverly's working names."

David Shapiro was quiet for a moment. "I've shot a lot of women over the years with names like that—Candy, Mandy, Dandy, but I never forget a face. I would have recognized Beverly if she'd ever been one of my models . . . and nah, Annie never mentioned her. We don't talk much."

His statements rang true. As voluble as he was, the volume of his music would impede conversation during the photo shoots. He hadn't even told Annie that he'd discovered Beverly's body.

"Thanks. I have to get back to tracking down the bad guys."

"Wait a minute," he whined. "What about my needs?"

I laughed.

"Look, Carol, I have a friend in the P.I. business. I could arrange for you to start logging those training hours you need for your license."

This guy knew how to hone in for the kill.

# CHAPTER 27

Now that I'd eaten, showered, and transformed myself into a sweet-scented, stunning sex machine, the first man I encountered was a grease monkey at the 76 Station, a rail thin man with gray tufts of hair.

"No nail. No hole. No leak. Someone must've let the air out of your tire," he said.

From there, I continued down Soquel Drive on my way to Spa Fitness. The up side of the increased traffic lights and congestion was more time for contemplation.

My mom had been right about the flat tire. If she were also right that the culprit had meant to detain me, who knew where I was going? David Shapiro had known I was trying to reach Annie. At the Crow's Nest, I'd asked him for her number. But how could he have known I'd be at the Hinds House unless he'd followed me from work? Even then, how could he have known I was on my way to Annie's? And why would he or anyone else want to prevent me from reaching Annie unless she'd known more about Beverly's murder than I'd extracted at the Catalyst? The questions kept me preoccupied through the crawl of traffic.

Anxiety began with a tickle in the base of my spine and ended with my fingers clenched around the steering wheel. Annie's busy phone. Annie not home.

Even on a Sunday evening, the Spa was a hopping place, voted Santa Cruz County's finest year after year in the *Good Times* poll. It had a reputation as the spot for singles in Spandex. If I had any sense and any money, I'd buy myself a leotard and join.

I circled the parking lot in back three times before a Mercedes backed out and I slid into the slot. In an exercise room off the passageway to the gym, a commander barked orders to a Spin class.

Since I didn't have any investigator's license to whip out, I was depending on the clerk's youth, inexperience, and general disinterest in anyone over thirty.

When I asked who'd been working the floor last Wednesday evening, he barely looked up. My painted lashes and lips had no effect on him. He swiveled in his chair, grabbed a clipboard with schedules, and thumbed through the pages as he continued to check in arriving patrons.

"Mike Taylor was in charge." He turned and hung up the clipboard.

"Who else was working?"

Now he looked up, brow furrowed. All of twenty-two with combed back dark hair and chest muscles pushing at his teal Spa Fitness shirt. "Mike Taylor would be the person to talk to."

The little shit simply didn't want to look through the papers again.

"Mike Taylor is the person I want to talk about, not the person I want to talk to."

The annoyance on his face shifted to mild interest. "Do you have a complaint?"

"No."

When I didn't add anything, his green eyes locked on mine, unaware that he'd taken on The Stare Down Queen. It was a cheap and hollow victory. The kid had no skill. He twirled in his seat and flipped the sheets without taking down the clipboard. "Irene Vargas."

"She working now?"

"Yeah. If you're a member, you can just go up and talk to her."

"Could you call Irene to the front desk?"

He cringed as if I'd asked him to lick my earwax. But he paged Irene. He waved a hand toward an array of couches. "You may want to sit over there. It's pretty busy. She may not be down for a while."

Contrary to his wishes, Irene came bouncing toward me in less than two minutes. She shook my hand firmly and pulled her brown ponytail tight. She wore a big smile; I could, after all, be a potential client.

I quickly disabused her of that notion.

"I already talked to the police."

"So you confirmed Mike Taylor's alibi?"

She pulled a bit on her Spa Fitness shirt and worked on making a perfect ledge over her black Spandex shorts. "We worked together. We got out of here about eleven."

The information sounded like a recitation. She sniffed the air. "I smell pipe tobacco."

"That's my lotion. Vanilla."

"Mike and I and two other women went to the Blue Lagoon."

This was a surprise. I couldn't picture Irene chumming with Mike Taylor. She looked so young and all-American in her rolled down white socks and athletic shoes.

"And you vouch for his whereabouts until the wee hours of the morning?"

"Not exactly." She glanced over her shoulder toward the hallway from whence she'd come. "As I told the cops, Mike was gone for a while. We saw him with some guy. They were hitting it off. We weren't paying a lot of attention."

"So he could have met Beverly Levandowsky?"

She shrugged.

I understood how mothers accidentally killed their babies by shaking them until their brains rattled in their skulls. I wanted to shake this bimbo until her ponytail unraveled. And it would have been intentional.

"How long was Mike away from your group?"

"I don't know. Maybe a half hour. After he left, some guys came over to our table and we were partying."

"So you really don't know how long he was gone?"

She shook her own ponytail.

So much for Mike Taylor's airtight alibi.

I used the pay phone in the hallway to call Annie's number. A guy answered and said she wasn't home.

"Have you seen her today?"

"No."

"Do you have any other housemates? Have any of them seen her?"

"No. I mean yes. There's another housemate, but no we haven't seen her. Shawn and I were just wondering what was up with her."

"Why's that?"

I tried to sound calm.

"I don't know. It just looked like she left in a hurry."

"How's that?"

"Who are you?"

This question always threw me into an existential quandary although the guy seemed satisfied with just my name. "I put a note for her under the mat."

"Oh, yeah, I picked that up," he said. "Well it's nothing, really, just she left the milk out and didn't take her cell phone. The weirdest thing is that she left the regular phone off the hook."

When I exited the gym, the fog had rolled in. The chilling mist collected on my bare arms and legs. I kept the back seat of my Ghia folded down and among the junk stashed in the compartment, I found an old gray sweatshirt. My stomach clenched as I drove to the Santa Cruz Police Department.

# CHAPTER 28

Even though the city was planning to relocate the police department, for now a large part of the SCPD occupied a squat brick building, the former telephone company headquarters for a much smaller Santa Cruz. The police had been crammed into the space since the 1989 earthquake.

"The infamous Carol Sabala," Homicide Detective John Carman greeted me. It was after six o'clock, but the creases in his dress shirt were stiff as meringue and the soft stripes contrasted handsomely with his dark hair and skin.

"Marriage looks like it agrees with you," I said, as he ushered me past the bulletproof glass into the inner sanctum, a warren of crowded, messy desks. It reminded me of the English Department at Watsonville High School where I'd done my last investigation.

Detective Carman turned a bit and grinned. "It does. But I'm not sure homicide investigation agrees with Alexis. Here I am on a Sunday evening. In her world, I should be home barbecuing steaks."

Detective Carman wore Levi's and his butt reminded me of Chad's. You should have married me, I thought. I like homicide investigations.

He led me into a dingy office and motioned to a chair by his desk. "So this has to do with the Beverly Levandowsky case."

"I'm here to tell you everything I know."

"Wise move." He sat and opened an already substantial file.

I rolled up the grease-stained cuffs of my gray sweatshirt and wrapped one leg around the other to try to warm my goose-bumped chill. So much for looking hot in the world of studs.

"Mind if I tape?" he asked. "I failed note-taking 101."

*Note-taking. Student. Professor. Sexually strange.*

"Are you okay, Carol?" Detective Carman asked. "You're shivering. Would you like some coffee?"

I shook my head. Could it be that my mom was right? Again?

I told Carman everything. I included information the police no doubt knew—the photos David Shapiro had taken, the Mr. Wrong ad, Mike Taylor's less-than-perfect alibi. I told him about Annie's connection to Beverly and my fear for her safety.

His smooth forehead wrinkled in concern, but I'd anticipated what he'd say. "Because of the homicide, we can certainly go to the house and ask questions, but even with that, we're limited in what we can do. She's not even a missing person yet."

I stopped shy of offering my free association, the connection between Annie and Klaus Holthuis and my mom's misgivings about the professor. I needed to talk to my mother. But first it was imperative that I change into some warmer clothes and collect my thoughts.

Detective Carman's kind face leaned toward me. "I'm probably wasting my time warning you, Carol, but this case is not like the other ones you've poked into. You need to stay out of this. We're not looking at a jealous boyfriend or a robbery gone bad. This guy is really dangerous."

# CHAPTER 29

When I unlocked the door to my house, the phone was shrilling. I sprinted to the bedroom, accidentally kicking Lola. Near tears, I answered, kneeling apologetically to stroke my cat.

"What's wrong, Carol?"

It was Chad. I wanted to say, "Everything." I wanted him to come over and to hold me. I wanted him to get out his baseball bat to protect me the way he'd once done. But I remembered his new girlfriend, young and cute in her Victoria's Secret lingerie. I remembered that at least on the surface, the divorce had been my idea.

"I'm working on a case," I said. "You know how that is." The words were designed to guard against any tenderness he was extending, to remind us both of how we'd met our demise. My obsessive investigating and Chad's obsessive concern. Oil and water.

"Yeah," he said, without rancor, "I remember."

The gentleness punctured my heart.

"I called to talk about the house," he said.

"I can't talk now." I slammed down the phone, turned into the quilt on my bed, and sobbed.

I made it a snappy little cry, since I had a phone message.

Uncle Teddy's voice instantly irritated and fortified me. How could my mom and her older brother Beanie be so tough, and Uncle Teddy be so sniveling?

"My visit to the Court Clerk's Office was certainly enlightening," he crowed. "This Klaus guy sounds like a real loser. Give me a call."

The last thing in the world I wanted to do was call Uncle Teddy. Why couldn't he have left a message? I diligently poked the numbers.

He answered on the second ring and wanted to chitchat. "How are you, Carol? How's your mom?"

"Tell me what you found out."

"Slow down a little. You always were such an impatient little girl, Carol."

I wanted to crawl through the phone line and strangle the passive-aggressive jerk. Was this how the murderer felt? Bursting with frustrated rage.

"There *was* a case," Uncle Teddy purred. "Last year, this guy Klaus tried to choke his live-in girlfriend. He was originally charged with felony spousal abuse, but the girlfriend flipped out and took off. Without her, the DA didn't have a case and the charge was reduced to a misdemeanor through diversion.

"Your mom was right to be worried. It's been my experience that she's always right. You should take her a little more seriously, Carol. Neither you nor Donald—"

I hung up. I dialed my mother's number and listened to the phone ring.

I changed into my black sweats faster than Clark Kent could rip off his suit. As usual when panicked, my mind ricocheted and I wondered what Clark Kent did with his suit. If he left it in the phone booth, wouldn't folks start to wonder about him?

I double-checked the wooden poles in my windows and sliding glass doors. I wished Chad's baseball bat remained in the closet or that the comforting heft of a nine millimeter Beretta pressed my palm. I had strong, steady arms and a good aim, but I'd decided against a gun because statistics said it was more likely to be used against me than in my defense.

I dashed to my car and drove like the Dukes of Hazzard. Unlike a Volkswagen bug, the Ghia cornered like a sports car and had no trouble going seventy. Ten minutes later, I squealed to a stop in front of the Hinds House, sprinted up the steps, and would have burst through the door except that it was locked.

# CHAPTER 30

Klaus Holthuis opened the door. Broad-shouldered and golden, he smiled. "Carol Sabala. All in black. You weren't very sociable this afternoon. I'm glad you've come back to visit."

My skin itched all over as though I had chicken pox. "Where's my mom?"

His forehead wrinkled and he stepped back to avert the blow of American rudeness. "I imagine she's in her room, avoiding what's left of the party."

*Then why hasn't she answered her phone?*

As I stepped onto the parquet floor, I realized Klaus was not alone. Alice Miller and another woman still sat sedately in the parlor. Both had steely looks aimed my way. The air was laden with wine, perfume and sexual competition.

In a concession to my knees, I raced up the steps one at a time, thinking about The Trial of the Century. The smooth, calm exterior of O.J. Simpson. A man who insisted upon, perhaps believed in, his innocence. If Klaus Holthuis were a murderer, he possessed the same uncanny ability.

*This guy is dangerous.*

Saint Francis did nothing to calm me. I pounded on my mom's door. The television reporter's indignation was turned down a notch and my mom said, "Carol?"

"Yeah. It's me. Open up."

"Good grief, child." My mom stood before me in a full-length flannel nightgown. "What's the matter?" She looked more like a grandma than a mother. Of course, if either of her children had bothered to reproduce, she would have been a grandma. She could even have been a great-grandma.

"Get on some clothes and pack a bag. You're coming to stay with me."

"Well aren't you a bossy frog."

I pushed past the white flannel dotted with pink roses and bumped my sore forehead on the slanted ceiling. "Damn it!" I held my head and wildly scanned the room for a suitcase or bag.

"I'm in the middle of watching *Sixty Minutes*. I really don't think anything is going to happen to me right here, right now."

Was my mom going senile? Had she forgotten her fear of Klaus Holthuis? Had I projected the quavering voice and vulnerable eyes earlier today?

Whatever the answers, Bea Sabala was probably right. Again. It was most annoying.

My sudden distrust of Klaus Holthuis was based on a misdemeanor charge that had not even kept him out of the university system. And even if he were capable of murder, he wasn't about to strangle anyone in the Hinds House on a Sunday evening when people occupied their rooms and visitors sat in the parlor.

But my mom was also right that I was stubborn. I pulled open the armoire, jerked her aqua warm-ups from a hanger and threw them on the bed. "Where is your underwear?"

"Why don't you go downstairs and talk to Klaus," she said, "while I pack my bag?" Although she slid open a drawer of the armoire, her eyes flicked back to the television.

"Are you serious?"

"Is the Pope Catholic?"

Leave it to my mom to use a twenty-year-old cliché to express sarcasm. But then, sarcasm didn't come naturally to her like it did to me. My mom was too serious for it.

"How are you going to learn about him if you don't talk to him?" she added. "He doesn't think *you* pilfered his mail. Just your dotty mom. He likes you," she said petulantly.

I wanted to tell her what I'd found out about Klaus Holthuis, but I preferred her to be crotchety rather than scared. "Are you sure, Mom, that you're not going to sit here and watch Andy Rooney talk about the wonder of paper clips?"

"This should take five minutes, Carol."

I left the room, but stood on the landing like a German shepherd watchdog.

Someone started up the steps. Even though the person walked slowly and lightly, the landing reverberated. The person paused on the second floor for a full minute. Then he continued to climb.

I pressed against my mom's door and rapped lightly.

"I said five minutes," my mom said peevishly. "Haste makes waste."

"Let me in," I whispered.

But it was too late. Klaus Holthuis had rounded the corner in time to witness the pitiful drama.

"Has Bea locked you out?" he asked, amused. "Let me see. Don't tell me." He snapped his fingers by his brain to summon the correct phrasing. "It's a mother/daughter thing." He smiled charmingly, pleased with his command of the vernacular.

I wanted to claw my way through the door. My eyes fastened on potential garrotes—his belt, the towel by the sink, whatever he was pulling from his pocket.

When my mom opened her door, I stumbled backward over her foot.

Klaus Holthuis laughed.

My mom yelped.

Klaus Holthuis stepped forward. He held a strap of leather with his keys on the end. "I'm sorry. I shouldn't laugh," he said. "But that was like your American Three Stooges." He extended his hand to help me up.

I didn't bite it. I accepted the strong, firm grip. "Are you taking a vacation?" he asked my mom, eyeing her overnight bag.

I willed. I prayed. I sent psychic messages to my mom. *Do*

*not tell this man where you are going.*

"I'm going to Ferndale for a few days. Homesick, I guess."

I stared, transfixed. Cut umbilical be damned. Some wires were never severed.

My mom had barely thrown her bag into the back of the Ghia and situated herself in the bucket seat before she laid into me. "What's the matter with you?" she asked harshly. "Did you want that man to know where we're going?"

"What did I do?"

"You stood there gawking."

"I didn't know you could lie like that." I gunned the Ghia up Chestnut. "You aren't going to Ferndale, are you?"

My mom sighed. "Bless your tiny heart." She patted me on the knee.

I felt like one of those perfectly preserved ancient artifacts that one touch could crumble to dust.

She had softened me for the kill. "If you want to become a private detective, I support you completely, and my offer of ten thousand dollars still holds, but, Carol, has *anyone* suggested that you might be too innocent to be a private detective?"

"I don't need this now, Mom. Watch and make sure we're not followed. Do you know what Klaus drives?"

"An old, orange BMW." My mom gripped her seat as though it could help her if I slammed on my brakes.

I filled her in on what I'd learned about Klaus from Uncle Teddy.

"This is what I need to know. That girl you told me about, the one you saw with Klaus when he had the handcuffs, what did she look like?"

"She was a pretty girl. Blonde."

"Green eyes?"

In the dark interior, my mom gave me a deprecating look and smacked her lips. "I didn't get that close."

"Was she about twenty?" I watched in the rearview for what I thought might be BMW headlights. Even on a Sunday night, this section of freeway was busy.

"I guess so. I could tell you better if I'd seen the inside of her mouth, but frankly, anymore, I can't tell sixteen from twenty-six."

"Was she in that range?" I sounded angry and impatient even to myself.

"Yes."

"Slender?" I checked the rearview.

"Yes."

"Did he ever call her Annie?"

"No. I think he called her 'dear' once."

"Well, you might be right." I strangled on the words. "Klaus could be the murderer."

# CHAPTER 31

As I turned off Morrissey onto Soquel and then off Soquel to the street that led to my cul-de-sac, no one followed us.

My mom had not boasted, "I told you so," but rather had pulled inward and become smaller like drying dentifrice. She had transformed, once again, into a frightened old lady.

My street was dead. I parked at the end of the cul-de-sac rather than in front of my house in the U. My neighbors on either side were a young renter, who worked all hours, and an elderly couple, who were in bed by eight. The light was on in Mrs. Brown's house across the street, but that was not necessarily comforting. She was an older widow reported to have visions. Every June she brought me a bag of plums from her tree and spoke with a thick accent I couldn't place.

My mom scurried behind me down the dark street.

At the door to the house, Lola greeted us. My mom, not a cat lover, stepped by her. "She's getting fat."

I locked the door and threw the deadbolt behind us.

My mom stood in the center of the small living room and looked around as though she were on the moon. She hadn't been in the house since my separation from Chad. The bare walls and plastic lawn furniture were a bit shocking. "Why didn't you tell me, Carol? I have enough stuff in storage to furnish this place twice over."

Asking my mom for help had never occurred to me. Even now at her suggestion, I saw a psychological maze—how to say no to the plaid couch, but yes to my grandma's round oak table.

I had no television to entertain my mom. No music to

calm her nerves. "Would you like to go to bed?" I asked.

"I'm not that old." She sat on one of the plastic chairs and rested her bag beside her. "Klaus doesn't know where you live, does he?"

I picked up Lola for comfort and sat across from her. "He might."

"He might?" she echoed. Even though the blinds were closed, she turned intently toward the front window, as though Klaus, if he were tracking us, would walk up to the front door.

"You know how you told him about me buying the house?"

"Yes. But I didn't tell him where you lived."

"I more or less told him." I stroked Lola, who contentedly made muffins against my stomach, unaware that our lives were endangered. "He was chatting me up about property in Santa Cruz."

"More or less?" my mom questioned.

"I told him the street."

My mom groaned and shrank. Given the short cul-de-sac, I may as well have given him the address. "Maybe we should check into a hotel."

"It's a thought. But what are we going to do, live there the rest of our lives? Eventually we'd have to come home."

I lapsed into a reverie on guns. I'd tested a Firestar M43 imported from South America. "American Firearms Industry's 1993 Handgun of the Year," the salesman had told me.

The gun had been narrower than most, with a single-stacked magazine rather than side-by-side rows of cartridges. This made the gun comfortable in my hand, as well as flatter and easier to conceal.

The phone rang, startling all of us. Lola sprang out of my lap.

"Is this the Republican with big hair?" David Shapiro asked.

"I can't deal with this right now." I hung up. I was

becoming quite proficient at this.

Within moments, the phone shrilled again. This guy was persistent. I turned down the ringer and closed the bedroom door.

"Who is that?" My mother's voice quavered. Suddenly it all seemed too much—the pulsing white walls, my frightened mother, the low screeching of the phone.

"Maybe you're right. Maybe we shouldn't stay here like sitting ducks."

The phone stopped ringing. Lola jumped into my mom's lap and she pushed the cat down. She smiled grimly. "Twice in one day. This must be a record."

"Twice in one day what?"

"I'm right."

I sat opposite her. "This is what I'm thinking. Instead of sitting here, working ourselves into a panic about Klaus and how he's coming to get us, we could, at least, make ourselves moving targets, and I could do a little more investigation."

"Why do you need to investigate if you already know who the murderer is?"

"I'm *not* one hundred percent sure who the killer is. What have we established? Even if I didn't know before that Klaus was hitting on Annie, I already knew that there was a connection between them, and that Annie knew Beverly."

"But you didn't know before that he tried to kill his girlfriend," Mom said. "And he likes bondage, and he let the air out of your tires, and now Annie is missing." My mom had given up attempting to see through the front blinds and now had her head craned toward the side window, straining to see beyond her reflection.

"Mom, that's not a good idea. As a matter of fact, I'm going to turn off the lights except the one above the stove. In case you don't remember, a killer once shot at me through the window."

"Well I guess I would prefer to be moving rather than sitting here in the dark," she said.

While I'd liked the feel of the nine-millimeter Firestar, I wished now for a revolver. Revolvers were simple, especially good when under stress and one didn't have extra seconds to figure out the complexities of a semi-automatic.

# CHAPTER 32

Other than guilt for locking Lola in the closet, I felt better zooming down the freeway in my car. I assigned my mom to watch for a tail again. Since the Ghia had a small back window and no passenger-side rearview, this kept her busy twisting and turning in her seat.

As the freeway turned to Highway 1 and we came to the first light, she reported, "There are several cars that have been behind us since Morrissey, but nothing that looks like his BMW."

"Good job, Mom."

We ascended the long hill, the beautiful old Holy Cross Church to our left, and then started the trudge down Mission Street. Even with the minimal traffic of a Sunday night, the street was a nightmare of lights, weird bends, and potholes.

"There are still three cars behind us that have been behind us since Morrissey."

This was not surprising. The freeway to Highway One/ Mission Street was the main way through Santa Cruz. I drove toward Annie's house.

"There was one car behind us for a long time," Mom said, "although I don't see it now. It wasn't an orange BMW."

I pulled to the curb at the flat-roofed, small house. The lights were out and it looked even more deserted than it had in the afternoon. "Do you know what kind of car it was?"

"White. Maybe a station wagon."

"Like a Ford Escort?"

"Subaru, Volvo, Ford, I couldn't tell you," my mom said.

"Do you know someone with an Escort?"

I didn't answer. David Shapiro knew Annie, and in spite of his protestations, he could have been acquainted with Beverly. My profile of the killer would include charming, convincing liar. So what if he had a state license to investigate? He wouldn't be the first person in law enforcement who'd turned out to be a killer. I opened the door of my car.

"Where are you going?"

"To see if anyone is home."

"No you aren't, young lady." She clutched my arm.

Even though I'd never been an obedient child, I closed the door.

My mom reached across me and locked it. "There could be a killer out there. Following us."

"There are lights on across the street and on both sides. Do you think he is going to strangle me here, in front of God and everyone?"

"He could shoot you."

"This guy gets his sexual jollies from strangling."

"Well excuse me all to pieces, but at this moment he may not be trying for *sexual jollies*." The word sexual rolled from her tongue with nary a tremble.

"Why did we drive all the way across town then?" I fumed silently for a minute. When I'd married Chad, I had not married my absent father, I'd married my mother. "Look, Mom, this is what I want to do with my life. It involves taking risks."

"You were always good at that," she said bitterly, relaxing her grip on my arm.

"The only question is whether you want to come with me or wait in the car."

"I'll wait here," she said, "but I'm going to sit in your seat. If I see Klaus, or anyone, I'll honk the horn. What does the guy with the white Escort look like?"

I described David Shapiro. For good measure, I threw in a thumbnail sketch of Mike Taylor.

"You know, Carol," she said in a last-ditch effort, "I don't understand why you have to do this."

I didn't understand my motivation fully, either, but it had something to do with my mother demanding that I stay.

I embodied a perverse and childish character flaw that had destroyed my marriage.

I need therapy, I thought, as I walked toward the darkened bungalow.

# CHAPTER 33

I rang the bell. The night was quiet and I listened for any movement behind the sheet curtains. The forlorn call of a foghorn resounded through the muffled chill.

Pressing the bell again, I faced the street to reassure my mom. The neighbors across the street had their drapes open, although nobody was in sight in the living room.

I lifted the clay pot with its dead plant. The key gleamed dully, slightly to the right of where I'd seen it earlier. I straightened quickly with a new rush of adrenaline, but then reminded myself that one of Annie's housemates could have used the key. I used my own spare frequently. Before illegally entering the premises, I decided to check out the grounds.

Leaving the porch, I turned past the two old bikes. The passage back to the detached garage was pitch black. I took a tentative step into the darkness, my hand outstretched. I might as well have had my eyes closed. This side yard was colder and damper than the front, as though it stayed in shade all day.

At the first blast of the horn, I jumped, wheeled, and tripped. I scrabbled frantically against long wet grass and damp earth, expecting a cord to loop about my neck. I remembered what I'd learned in self-defense and raised my shoulders to my ears. The posture provided a simple and effective obstacle to being choked, although it made for awkward running. I headed for the car, ducked low, in case the person opened fire.

I jerked open the door to the Ghia, only to find my mom in my spot. I ran to the opposite side and pulled at the locked door. "Mom!" I shouted in an adrenaline rush of panic. I twirled my head, looking for my attacker. I banged on the window.

She reached across and unlocked the door. I jumped into the passenger seat and pushed down the button. "Who did you see?" I slouched in the car and pulled down my mom's head at the same time.

My mom butted my hand from her head and jerked herself upright. "I didn't see anyone."

Anger pressed up from my core like red-orange lava. "God damn it, Mom!" I wiped damp dirt from the heel of my hands onto my jeans. "Did we, or did we not, agree that the horn was a signal if you saw someone?"

"You didn't say you were going back there."

"I didn't say I wasn't."

"I thought you were only going to the door. If I'd known you were going back there, I wouldn't have let you out of the car."

"Right, Mom, like you really could have prevented it."

"There's no reason to get snotty."

"Oh, right, again, Mom. Just because I fell in the mud and had visions of dying and my adrenaline shot through the roof, that's no reason to be angry."

She sat quietly for a minute. "You know, you got this temper from your great Grandpa Turner."

"Do you think you could give my genetic defects a rest?"

She remained silent and we both looked around. A man stood inside the house across the street and seemed to be peering right at us through his uncovered window. The sight was both mortifying and reassuring.

"Why do you want to go back there and look, anyway?"

"I suppose it's some sort of illogical intuition I received from my father's side." This preemptive strike seemed mean spirited, but I didn't retract it or say I was sorry. I only kicked myself for not leaving her in the Hinds House. She'd been content to watch *Sixty Minutes* and go to bed. With her door locked, she probably would have been safer there than here with me.

"Do you have a flashlight in the car?" She was caving in, giving me permission to go, beating me to the punch before I could spitefully point out that she was the one who'd offered me ten thousand dollars to find out about Klaus Holthuis.

"I do." I twisted and rummaged in the back compartment. Chad had gotten the good flashlight; he'd bought it. Besides, he was the one who kept up with things like tightening washers and replenishing batteries.

"I won't beep unless I see someone," my mom promised.

"Good." I tested the flashlight, which had been rolling around in my hot, dusty car for the last year. It cast a dim light. "You don't want to come with me?"

"I think this is better."

I thought so, too. Armed with a flashlight, I once again headed for the forbidding tunnel.

The pale yellow globe of light revealed huge hydrangea bushes to my left and a redwood fence to the right. Two tracks of concrete with overgrown grass in the middle led to the garage doors. They opened outward from a hasp in the middle. There was no padlock, but the doors had collapsed onto the latch. To open them, I'd need both hands and all my strength to lift.

I shone the dim light in a full circle, trying to figure out the most useful place to set the flashlight. Even though the side yard was overgrown, it was remarkably free of junk. I balanced the flashlight on a window ledge aimed toward the back, although the orb missed the garage completely.

It didn't matter much. Now that I had the lay of the land, it was almost as though I could see. I shuffled to the garage, put my shoulder to a door, lifted the clasp, and dragged the door open, scraping over the buckled concrete path.

The blast of the horn startled me. I stumbled to the flashlight. When I reached for it, it slid from its precarious perch and hit the ground. Impenetrable darkness closed around me.

# CHAPTER 34

I retreated from where the flashlight had last beamed. That's where a person would expect me to be. The honking horn effectively masked the rustling and snapping of the hydrangea bushes. I hoped the noise would also alert some neighbors. Trapped in sheer and utter darkness, I backed around the corner of the house.

The blare of the horn stopped.

"Are you okay?" a familiar voice called out.

*Come on, Mom, do something.*

I heard the roar of my Ghia's engine. *Is she leaving me? Going for the cops?* My heart sank.

Then the driveway was flooded with light and my mom was screaming, "Freeze or I'll run right over you."

Illuminated by the Ghia's lights, David Shapiro stretched his arms to the side and dropped the revolver he held.

As if to indicate her seriousness, my mom revved the engine.

"I was following you to make sure you were okay," David Shapiro yelled. "I could tell something was wrong when I called."

I cautiously crept around the corner. "Kick the gun toward me."

He complied.

"How did you know where I lived?" I moved forward and snatched up the gun. It looked like a common thirty-eight caliber Colt Detective Special. Here was living proof of the statistics that said a gun was more likely to be used against you than to protect you.

"I'm an investigator, Carol. Remember?"

"Why were you investigating me?"

"Hasn't that been obvious since day one?"

I pointed the gun at him.

"I wish you wouldn't do that," he said calmly.

"You're the one who brought it. Didn't you expect to use it?"

"Maybe. But not on you."

"Move toward the garage."

He inched forward. "What are you going to do, Carol?"

"Stay behind him in the car, Mom."

The Ghia rolled menacingly toward David Shapiro. The image of my mom driving into the post office filled my mind.

"Now that I've gone through all this trouble, I just want to see if there's anything in the garage." I conjured up images of Annie strung from a noose, meant to disguise her strangulation as a suicide or autoerotic asphyxia. "Pull open that other door."

As the door grated across the concrete, the headlights revealed built-in tables topped by pegboard along both walls. A surfboard lay on top of one table and a wet suit hung from a hanger hooked into the pegboard. Under one bench was a box and an army trunk. It was the emptiest garage I'd ever seen.

"Satisfied?" David Shapiro asked.

"I won't be satisfied until we peek inside that trunk."

"Stop right there," said a voice behind us.

# CHAPTER 35

"Drop the gun."

I gladly followed the orders since I could see they didn't come from Klaus, but rather from a Santa Cruz police officer with his gun drawn.

"Please step out of the car," his partner commanded my mom.

"Should I turn it off?" my mom asked in a trembling voice.

"Put it in neutral and set the brake. We can use the light."

"Bob?" David Shapiro said, turning slowly.

"Well, I'll be God damned," the officer named Bob said. "David Shapiro? Who's the lady with the gun?"

"She's my trainee," he said smoothly. "Carol Sabala."

I felt chagrined that the officer knew David, but not me. I'd thought that my involvement in two previous investigations had made me a legend.

"I thought she was threatening you," the first officer said.

"It's my gun," David Shapiro said. "I can show you the license."

"That won't be necessary," Officer Bob said. "I know you're licensed."

"Who are you?" the first officer barked at my mom. He kept his gun drawn and ready. He wasn't buying the all-in-the-family, everything's-hunky-dory spin.

"I'm Bea Sabala, Carol's mom."

"What are you doing here?"

She sighed wearily. "I came with my daughter."

"To do what?" he growled. "We had a call for a B&E."

"Is this place a community care facility?" Officer Bob asked hopefully, wanting this all to play out in a nice, peaceful way, wanting David to have a legitimate reason for poking around on the property.

As David hesitated for a second, debating whether to lie, Officer Bob pivoted suddenly toward a figure running across the front yard.

"Duuuude. What's going on? Did you guys find Annie? Is she okay?"

"Stop right there!" the officer with the gun commanded.

The young man stepped into the light and seeing the gun, threw his hands half way into the air. Long shorts rode low on his narrow hips and his gangly legs ended in a pair of enormous Teva sandals.

"Who are you?" the officer asked.

"Whoooa. I'm Ryan Riordan. I live here."

"Ryan, I spoke to you earlier," I inserted. "I'm Carol Sabala."

"Oh, yeah. Annie still hasn't come home." He had the face of a ten-year-old—smooth skin, sun-burnt nose and freckles, all covered with a patina of worry.

"Do you know this woman?" The officer with the gun relaxed.

"I don't know her, know her, but we talked on the phone. She's searching for my housemate Annie, who is missing."

"I talked to Detective Carman about this matter earlier this evening," I reported to the cop.

Appearing ready to holster his gun, he asked Ryan, "Did you make a call about a possible breaking and entering?"

Ryan shook his head.

If police officers arrived on a scene and there were no obvious drugs, no theft, no broken bones, bullet wounds or dead bodies, and they could leave without writing an incident report, that's what they'd prefer. They were supposed to write up every time they drew a weapon, but who knew? Most people didn't become cops because they had a love of composition in high school.

Ryan glanced, puzzled, at the jacked-open garage doors.

"Was someone trying to steal my surfboard?" He finally felt free to lower his arms. His eyes roved the circle of the five of us and found us unlikely candidates.

"I had this hunch about Annie," I volunteered.

"You thought you'd find her in there?" Ryan's voice broke. "Like a body?"

"I'd still like to take a look inside that trunk."

Ryan's expression was that of someone startled by impending vomit. "That's just my fins and masks and snorkeling stuff."

"Would you be willing to open it?" Officer Bob asked. "Then maybe we can clear all this up and get on with our business."

# CHAPTER 36

The trunk contained exactly what Ryan had claimed. He was visibly relieved not to discover a chopped-up body.

I felt like an idiot. Annie's Cabriolet was not here. Why had I expected her body to be here? The murderer was too smart to let himself be seen at her house. He would have called her to meet him. But then why was the phone off the hook?

"Do you want to charge these people with breaking and entering?" the officer asked.

Ryan shook his head. "I'm really worried about Annie. If she still isn't home tomorrow, I'm going to call her parents."

"That's a good idea," Officer Bob said. He yawned and turned to go, but the other officer seemed reluctant to leave Ryan with a band of wackos.

So, we stood in the chilly driveway conducting a postmortem of the evening, as though we'd all attended a complicated and pretentious dance piece and none of us wanted to admit we didn't understand it. As the night wore past midnight, I became convinced that David Shapiro had followed me to watch my back. I just wasn't sure how I felt about it. When he asked if my mom and I would like to go for a bite to eat, I snapped, "No."

"Does no mean yes?" he asked.

Mom glared at him as though he were the Antichrist.

Finally the other housemate Shawn pulled to the curb in a boat of a station wagon, and tripped toward us over the lawn, followed by a cloud of marijuana fumes.

"Dude, what's up?" he asked Ryan.

"It's a long story." Ryan steered his friend toward the house, the cue for the end of the party. David Shapiro walked down the sidewalk toward his hidden car. The police sat in their patrol car at the curb.

My mom and I sank wearily into the Karmann Ghia. Thank God tomorrow was Monday. While much of the world dreaded Mondays, bakeries typically closed that day. Archibald's still cranked out a limited supply of muffins and bread, but it was my day off.

I turned off the car engine, worried about how much juice had been sucked from its battery.

"What are you doing?" my mom asked. "Those policemen are waiting for us to leave."

"I know. But I want to talk to Ryan and Shawn some more."

"I don't think that's a good idea."

"What are they going to do? Arrest me? There's no law against it."

"There's no law against driving your car over a cliff, either," my mom muttered.

"Come with me. It'll look more innocent."

As we climbed from the car, the two officers watched us. We'd already rung the doorbell by the time they got out of their patrol car. Ryan promptly opened the door. "You're still here," he said.

The two policemen joined us on the porch. "We expected you folks to go on home and to leave these two young men alone. I think we've all had enough excitement for one night."

"Actually, Officer . . . ," Ryan squinted to read his name tag, ". . . Dodd, I'd like to know what she wants."

"I want to know how Annie's room looks. If there are any other signs that she left hurriedly or unwillingly."

He opened the door wider. "That's just what Shawn and I were trying to figure out. If you want to help us with Annie, you can come in."

The invitation was to all four of us. My mom and I stepped onto the worn wood floor, but the two officers hesitated on the porch. They'd witnessed Ryan invite us into his home, so there wasn't anything they could do to prevent us from entering. On the other hand, they had no official business here. Ryan had not pursued a B&E charge and Annie was not a missing person, yet.

"If you're sure you're okay, Mr. Riordan, we'll be on our way," Officer Dodd said.

Ryan had clearly hoped the two officers would accept his invitation, but instead he was stuck with just my mom and me. The three of us watched as the cops slowly made their way to their vehicle, giving Ryan plenty of time to call them back, to ask for their assistance in ridding the house of our pestilence. Instead he shouted, "Maybe you guys could keep an eye out for her car. A white Cabriolet. License plate number," he pulled a paper from his pocket, "2SEA187." His mammoth sandals slapped the pavement as he ran after them and handed Officer Bob the paper. "Oops, oops, wait up. I want to give you our phone number."

"I have a pen," Officer Bob volunteered and jotted down Ryan's number.

"You can call at any time," Ryan said.

*What a sweet guy.* There was no hint of romantic involvement between him and Annie and yet he seemed completely concerned about her, as though she were a treasured younger sister.

As Ryan shut the door, my focus turned toward the inside of the house. My place was more cheerful. The amount and quality of furniture was about equal, but at least my doors and windows and floors were in good shape.

Shawn emerged from one of the rooms off the hallway. "Everything looks cool." His rumpled tee shirt and messy hair made him look like he'd gotten out of bed.

"Is that her room?" I asked.

He waved us back. The room was small and neat with the wall opposite the door painted a deep mauve.

"She said that color was supposed to promote sleep," Ryan explained over my shoulder.

Annie's bed was a futon on the floor.

My mom pointed at the quilt. "Drunkard's Path."

The two boys stared at her.

"That's the quilt's pattern," I explained.

My mom knew the patterns, but preferred crazy quilts, a bit like abstract painting with no discernible pattern. The quilt she'd made for me, with irregular squares and strips of forest green and dusty rose, was one of my favorite possessions. I wondered who had made this quilt for Annie. A grandmother perhaps. It didn't look like anything one could buy at Mervin's.

From the mauve wall a poster of Albert Einstein and another of P.J. Harvey stared at us, but the screen saver on the computer pulled my attention to the side of the room. It was a naked photo of Annie that splintered and fractured in various ways and then momentarily regrouped to give one an eyeful of Annie.

Our group spread into the room. The dresser supported an array of candles and cosmetics, a packet of birth control pills, and a single vase full of white daisies.

"Do you mind?" I put my hand on the knobs of the dresser drawer.

"Go ahead," Shawn said. "I already looked."

The top drawer held her socks and underwear, nothing racier than the thongs I'd seen her wearing at David Shapiro's. At the bottom of the drawer was a rubberbanded stack of twenty and one-hundred-dollar bills.

"Money from her modeling," Ryan said.

"So you guys knew about that?" I replaced the cash and patted my way through the tee shirts and shorts in the next drawer.

"It wasn't exactly a secret," Ryan said sarcastically, nodding at the screen saver.

My mom meandered to the closet, probably so she wouldn't have to see the monitor. The closet door had been replaced with strings of beads.

"Did Annie have a boyfriend?" I asked.

The third drawer of the dresser contained folded pants and

shirts and a vibrator. I felt a growing urgency to find a clue, something that would point to Annie's whereabouts.

"She used to go with my best friend Paul," Shawn said with a trace of bitterness. He shoved at his dark, lank bangs with the heel of his hand. He sat at Annie's desk and pawed through the drawer.

"What happened to that relationship?" The last dresser drawer held sweatshirts and sweaters and no surprises.

"She said he smoked too much dope." Pencils rolled and paper clips rattled. "But I think she met someone else."

"When did this happen?"

"At the start of the summer session."

"Any idea who the guy was?"

"She was really secretive," Ryan said. "I was worried that she was involved with someone older. Maybe married."

"Definitely someone who had control over her," Shawn drawled. He moved the mouse and clicked one of the icons. "I'm going to check her e-mail."

"It's password protected," Ryan said.

Shawn shot him a glance that said he was a moron. He clicked on the keys.

"You dog." Ryan moved to Shawn's shoulder.

"Paul told me."

While the e-mail loaded, I peered over my mom's shoulder. She finished slipping hangers along the bar of the closet. Lifting a brow, she held up a little leather skirt for me to see.

"Oh, dude, this is too pathetic," Shawn crooned.

We hurried to his side. "Paul's still writing her."

Shawn had opened the message and we all read Paul's sincere, sad declaration of undying love.

"Would he be obsessed enough to kidnap her?" I asked.

"I've been with him all day," Shawn said. "He couldn't have anything to do with Annie's disappearance. He didn't say anything about this, though." He clicked shut the window. "I have to talk to that young man."

"Click on that PussyTech message," I said. Anxiety was welling in me. I did not have a good feeling about Annie's safety.

*Hi Doll. I don't have any good advice about this guy. If you're getting a weird vibe, go with your gut. All that other stuff, how he's a dreamboat and a professor, that don't mean shit. That's just your brain trying to rationalize your in-and-out urge. Maybe the Mr. Wrong ad was no joke. Be cool. Be safe. You're my Numero Uno now.*

I bit my lip. I appreciated Cole trying to warn Annie even if he were motivated only by a desire to protect his merchandise.

"I think we need to pay a visit to Klaus Holthuis," I announced to the room.

"Now?" my mom asked, as the two boys simultaneously asked, "Who?"

"Right now," I said. "And I hope we're not too late."

# CHAPTER 37

I would have preferred to be in my Ghia, but we'd decided to go together. Shawn drove his surf mobile and I rode shotgun. Ryan had armed himself with Annie's cell phone. After I'd explained who Klaus was, we debated calling 911.

"It's better to be safe than sorry," my mom argued.

"There's four of us." Steering with one hand, Shawn cocked a bicep.

"What would we say?" Ryan asked. "We don't know if he has Annie."

I swung around to face him. "He probably won't have her there," I said. "Even with the party, it would have been hard to get her up to his room unnoticed." *Not to mention that he is too clever to contaminate his room with forensic evidence.* I doubted Annie had ever made it beyond the hallway where my mom had seen the two of them together.

"So why are we even going there?" Shawn asked.

"Because he *might* have her. Or he might lead us to her." *And she might still be alive.*

"So what should I tell the dispatcher?" Ryan persisted.

My mom glared at him. "You can tell him anything." I thought she was going to rip the phone from Ryan's hand. "It's easier to apologize than to get permission."

I didn't want to dampen their vigilante mood, but I felt sick, with growing certainty we were too late. And it seemed like my fault. Klaus must have panicked as soon as he'd seen me with Annie at the Catalyst. That's why he'd hurled me into the fence and tried to kill me.

Annie knew that Klaus was Mr. Wrong, probably from responding to the ad herself. And I think she'd pieced together that Beverly had answered it, too.

When Klaus saw me with the circled ad at the party, he must have felt the noose begin to tighten, the control begin to slip away, as it did with his victims.

Ever the thinker, Klaus had deflated my tires and then borrowed the car of his colleague Alice Miller to zip up to Annie's house. There he had persuaded her to drop everything and to follow him to God knows where. He'd taken the phone off the hook so that Annie wouldn't be pulled back to the house by the ringing—irresistible to someone barely out of her teens. And so there wouldn't be any urgent messages from me for the housemates to hear. If you interrupt communication, you can buy time. He'd bought himself most of an afternoon.

Shawn pulled his boat to a red curb near the Hinds House. We tumbled from the station wagon. My mom jerked the phone from Ryan's hand. "How do you work this thing?"

"Wait," I commanded.

They halted on the sidewalk like good soldiers. I'd never been in downtown Santa Cruz at two in the morning. It was serenely quiet and eerie. Not a single light burned in a window. Not a single vehicle cruised the streets. "We have to have a plan."

"I'm calling 911," my mom said.

"No, you're not. You have to knock on Klaus's door."

"Why me?"

"You're the only one who could be legitimately knocking, who wouldn't completely rouse his suspicion."

"I'm supposed to be on vacation."

"Something came up. Now you're locked out of your room." I moved toward the front door.

"If I'm going along with this hairball scheme, then I for sure want to call 911." We crept up the front steps and my mom quietly unlocked the front door.

"Ryan can do that," I whispered. "Then I want you guys to wait on the second-floor landing of the steps. He won't be able to see you, but you should be able to hear everything."

"Shouldn't we wait for the police?" Ryan asked.

"We probably *should*," I conceded, but even as my brain told me Klaus would not take Annie to his room, I pictured her on his bed, willingly bound and gagged, thinking she were about to have the best sex of her life. Then slowly, as he didn't undress, as he didn't kiss her, as she lay there longer and longer, her anticipation turning to wild-eyed fear.

I headed for the steps with my mom right behind me. Below us, the phone beeped three times as Ryan tapped in 911.

When we reached the top floor, there was no need for my mom to knock on Klaus's door. He stepped from his room onto the landing. Leather pants gripped his package and an old-fashioned swimming cap gripped his skull. One arm was draped with a towel. The revealed one was completely smooth, hairless as a newborn.

"Good evening, ladies," he said. "Or I guess I should say good morning."

Klaus dug into his tight pants and extracted the thin leather strap with his keys.

I backed up, my armpits trickling wet. "What are you doing?" My hand flew protectively to my throat.

He looked at me strangely. "I know that it might seem paranoid, but I lock my room when I go for a shower." The swimming cap eliminated the golden hair and threw his face into high relief. The lips were cruel and the eyes gleamed.

"A shower at two in the morning?" I tried to keep my voice neutral. *More like a shower to wash away evidence.*

"Normally I wouldn't want to wake Bea," he said solicitously. "But I thought she'd left for a vacation."

"I came back for my statue," my mom said. "Can you believe that? Halfway to Ferndale and I came all the way back," she prattled as she bent and hefted Saint Francis into her arms.

"He's good luck. I never go anywhere without him."

Klaus's cold eyes shifted between my mother and me. He stroked the leather cord. "Such a beautiful neck. And black becomes you, Carol. Isn't it interesting how the color for death is also the sexiest color? Black leather, black satin, black lace, black lingerie."

While Klaus drew from his enormous, unfailing reservoir of charm, a blur of yellow, blue and red flashed behind his head, followed by a crack. A blue chunk of concrete flew into my shin and I recoiled in pain. Klaus stared at me for a moment as though astonished at how silly I looked hopping on one leg and screaming, "Ow, ow, ow."

Then Klaus Holthuis toppled to the floor.

# CHAPTER 38

Officer Bob and his partner located Annie's Cabriolet in a downtown-parking garage. There was no sign of a disturbance, but when Annie remained missing, I held little hope. And I blamed myself.

I was glad that Ryan and Shawn had come with us that night. Their youthful energy kept us going during the questioning that lasted until dawn. With four of us telling a consistent story, the police had finally released us. Besides, my mom didn't fit the profile for a violent assault.

We'd been able to persuade the police to take Klaus's keys and leather strap as they were in plain view and we'd felt threatened by the strap. Since our case against Klaus was circumstantial, luckily the design on the strap looked like a match to the marks on Beverly's neck. It had been enough to convince the police to post a guard outside Klaus's hospital room.

Fortunately, I didn't have to work that Monday. But Tuesday was no better. I could barely drag myself from bed.

Suzanne patted me on the back and considered me a heroine, but it was small consolation. She had Hamad, and her life was moving away from mine. She'd probably desert me and set off on an adventure in Kuwait. I couldn't depend on her for comfort. In the end, I had only myself and I had to make what had happened right with myself.

My mom insisted on giving me a cashier's check for ten thousand dollars. "For the house only." She restrained herself from any comment about how right she'd been about Klaus, about investigating, about her ugly statue. I realized when it came to me, my mom probably practiced a great deal more restraint than I gave her credit for. "I want you to have your grandma's table," she declared. "I know you like it."

I did indeed. It was a round oak table with four solid matching chairs. My mom knew me better than I wanted to admit.

"You're welcome to the other stuff, too, although I sold the fuddy-duddy plaid furniture."

Annie's body turned up three days later, discovered by a couple of horseback riders on old Fort Ord. The deserted military base, in the process of conversion, was another favorite dumping ground.

Even though the remains were badly decomposed, the autopsy revealed that she'd been strangled. I felt confident concrete evidence would emerge to prove that Klaus Holthuis had committed both crimes in spite of the precautions he'd taken to eliminate hair and fibers. I wouldn't be surprised if eventually the police located the body of his missing girlfriend from Humboldt County.

For the present, Klaus Holthuis was nursing a major head injury and pleading innocent.

David Shapiro called and invited me on a bike ride. I felt too beaten up to resist. I dug my blue Schwinn from the storage shed, hefting it over paint cans and gardening equipment. I brushed off the cobwebs and rode it to the corner gas station to fill the tires with air. Herlindo, the attendant, came out to talk to me. About thirty years old, he was always neatly groomed, said "Thank you" to the customers and knew how to count change. He was worth more than the gas station could be paying him, which made me suspect he lacked documents.

"I saw your name in the paper," he announced.

*Literate, too,* I added to my list of praises.

"You're really brave knocking that guy out," he said.

"Actually my mom cold cocked the bastard."

"You're getting famous, Carol."

A suspect for the Beverly Levandowsky murder had, of course, been front-page news. My mom and I as well as Shawn and Ryan had been given lavish coverage. But neither the press nor Herlindo's accolades lifted my spirits.

I pedaled down Soquel Drive to David Shapiro's house.

"So your mom crushed the guy's skull?" David Shapiro asked enthusiastically. He wheeled my three-speed toward front steps spread with an array of biking supplies—helmet, pump, gloves, and sunglasses.

How was it, I wondered, that he had gained control of my bike? And why did I mind? *Less work for me.* Let him push the damn thing to Timbuktu.

"She would have been doing the world a favor. He must have a hard head. All he suffered was a concussion."

"Typical German," David muttered. "The only surprise is that the statue didn't crack in half."

"It lost a hand." If he were half as intent on me as he were on my bike, he would have noticed the golf-ball sized lump and bruise on my shin.

"This kickstand has gotta go," he said.

"What's wrong with it?"

"Extra weight. It probably weighs a pound."

"It doesn't bother me."

"How many people, Carol, do you see riding around with kickstands, except for little kids?"

*Judging by his tone, no one in the world but me.* "What do you do, then, when you get off the bike?"

"Put it in a stand, or do this." He laid my bike on its side.

I picked up the Schwinn and experimentally lowered it onto the dried-up crab grass.

"Not like that," he said.

Mystified, I looked at the bike. I'd been gentle. Certainly I wasn't crushing any valuable flowers.

He picked up the bike and laid it down.

I watched closely for the difference in methodology.

"The chain goes up. You want to protect the gears and bottom bracket."

Since the day I'd stayed balanced and upright, I'd thought I'd learned how to ride a bike, but apparently there was a lot more to it.

David Shapiro strode to his garage, returned with a toolbox and set to work dismantling the kickstand. "Try this for a week. If you don't like it better, I guarantee I'll put the kickstand back on for you."

I didn't have the heart to tell him that I hadn't ridden my bike for the last year, and wouldn't be riding it now if it weren't for his coercion.

He put the parts to the kickstand in a brown bag and handed it to me. "Feel that. Just feel how heavy it is."

"Thanks," I said dubiously.

"Did you read this morning's paper?"

I shook my head. Every time I looked at the coverage, I thought of Annie—her youth, her prettiness, her business major and pursuit of foreign languages, her whole life before her.

"One of the homeless identified Klaus from a photo as the guy he saw walking with a woman on the levee the night of the murder."

David took it upon himself to clean and oil my chain. "I guess you don't want to discuss the case."

"It's too depressing. If it weren't for me, Annie might still be alive."

"If it weren't for you, Klaus Holthuis might not have been arrested, and he wasn't going to stop with one victim. I wonder if Beverly was his first. I bet there are some unsolved homicides back in his part of Germany."

"Still, I don't think he would have chosen Annie if he didn't feel pushed to it. She was too connected to him and he was too smart to go after someone linked to him."

"He attacked his live-in girlfriend."

"True."

"Serial killers are often smart, Carol, but they're also cocky. We can't second guess what Klaus Holthuis might have tried."

From high in the yard's sycamore, a mockingbird ran through its repertoire. David Shapiro squeezed the bike's tires and found them satisfactory. "I know a route from here, almost twelve miles with hardly any surface streets."

"Twelve miles!" I worried about my knees.

"You'll do fine, although it would certainly be easier with a different bike. You don't even have cages for your pedals. A basic Trek would only cost a few hundred dollars."

"I just bought a house."

He donned wrap-around sunglasses, a black helmet and gloves. He looked like Darth Vader. "Check out my bike." He scooped it from the porch. With its gunmetal frame, rugged fat tires, and fancy components, it looked like a machine to take into battle.

He had me lift his bike and then lift mine. "Now I'm doubly worried about keeping up."

"You'll be fine." He swung himself onto his bike and took off up the street.

I pedaled furiously, cutting through the schoolyard, sweating, running stop signs, careening down the steep hill into the harbor. My hair whipped behind me. I grinned like a dog with its head out the window. The descent, the watch for cars, the effort to keep up demanded my full attention. There was no space to wallow in my guilt.

A light breeze tinged the boats' riggings against their masts. I was a freewheeling queen, ten again.

We turned right, made a hairpin turn, and climbed a dirt path into a wild, undeveloped area. The grass was high and gold, the hill dotted with live oaks. We stopped to look out over the harbor.

"This is spectacular. I've never been here."

"It's called Arana Gulch."

He extracted his water bottle and offered me a sip. "You must get a water bottle and a bracket."

"That I think I can afford."

I followed David around Arana Gulch and down along the harbor to a funky restaurant called Aldo's. People flocked to it in order to eat breakfast or lunch on a deck overlooking the mouth of the harbor.

We retraced our tracks and sped down the other side of the harbor, past the Crow's Nest, up through a quiet neighborhood, along busy Seventh Avenue, and into the parking lot of the new Simpkin's Swim Center, the pride of Live Oak.

In back of the center, we entered a wild, wooded area with dirt paths. *Twin Lakes State Park* an unobtrusive sign announced. We stopped to rest at Schwann Lake. I lay my bike on the dirt, chain up, and David and I squatted on a bluff. The softly slanted light hinted of autumn. Recumbent limbs framed the murky green and across the lake we could see the ocean. Ducks floated by and frogs plopped.

Life stilled and went on.

###

If you enjoyed *Rotten Dates*, please tell a friend about the book or consider posting a review on Amazon or Goodreads. Check out other Carol Sabala mysteries available as e-books or paperbacks. For more information about the author, visit www. vinniehansen.com.

# ACKNOWLEDGMENTS

A big thank you to Carol and Al Vogan, my sister and brother-in-law, for their feedback on the first draft of *Rotten Dates* and for firearms facts. My mom, Vivian Hansen, deserves credit as my Midwest distributor. My husband, Daniel Friedman, supplies information about Community Care Licensing. My Karmann Ghia connection is Dennis Farr at www.geocities.com/kg_faq. I am indebted to my sister-in-law Gwynn Hansen, former probation officer, and Steve Fabian, Esq. for tidbits about the California judicial system. Finally, this book would not exist without the guidance and wisdom of the ladies at misterio press.

# ABOUT THE AUTHOR

Vinnie Hansen fled the South Dakota prairie for the California coast the day after high school graduation.

A reading addict since childhood, Vinnie is now the author of the Carol Sabala mysteries. The seventh installment in the series, *Black Beans & Venom,* was a finalist for the Claymore Award. She's also written many published short stories including *Novel Solution* in the anthology, *Fish or Cut Bait,* and *Bad Connection,* the 2015 winner of the Golden Donut Award.

Still sane after 27 years of teaching high school English, Vinnie has retired and lives in Santa Cruz, California, with her husband and the requisite cat.

**VINNIEHANSEN.COM**

## Forget a Shaky Date; Enjoy a Date Shake

You may associate dates with the Mideast, but in fact 90% of the world's dates are grown in California's Coachella Valley. As a result, Palm Springs and the surrounding area have become famous for their date shakes.

Most of these shakes are high calorie concoctions made with ice cream. However, it's easy and simple to mix up a very healthy and super delicious date shake. Here's a recipe for one serving:

3 Medjool dates, pitted and diced
1 frozen banana cut into cubes
½ cup almond milk (unsweetened)
½ cup very cold milk
¼ tsp. vanilla

Throw the ingredients in a blender and blend until most of the lumps are gone. Serve and enjoy immediately.